He'd never felt anything like her

Never this soft, this silky, this alive. His chest tightened and his body responded on such a basic level that it was almost painful for him. When her tongue touched his lips, the tension grew. A tension he'd come to fear. He knew it had been too good to last that he could touch her without fear. He'd been a fool.

When he jerked his hand back, he braced himself for the emptiness. But he was wrong, as wrong as he'd been thinking he could trust himself to touch her. Harley stepped close, and he felt the warmth of her breath on his face. "Mitch, what's happening?"

He stared at the ceiling. There were no words left in him—not even lies.

Her hair fell around them, forming a dark curtain that included just the two of them in its protection. It closed off the world and everything of no consequence right then. "Mitch," she breathed, her voice hoarse with desire, "I...want you."

All he wanted was to pull her to him and know her completely. But all he could do was lie there. Lie there and curse himself for the mistake he'd made...the mistake that would never allow him to touch her.

Dear Reader,

You've made the MORE THAN MEN books some of your favorites, so we're bringing you *more!* Just as before, whether their special powers enable them to grant you three wishes or to live forever, these men's greatest power is that of seduction.

Mary Anne Wilson brings you the story of Mitch Rollins, a research scientist who injects himself with a serum that gives him superhuman strength. Unable to control his power, how can he do what we all take for granted—hold the one he loves?

Mary Anne makes her home in Southern California, far from the icy northwest setting of this book. But she knows what it's like to embrace her loved ones. Her entire family lives nearby.

So turn the page—and be seduced by Mitch. It's an experience you'll never forget!

Thank you for your letters—and be on the lookout for upcoming MORE THAN MEN books.

Regards,

Debra Matteucci
Senior Editor & Editorial Coordinator
Harlequin Books
300 East 42nd Street
New York, NY 10017

Mary Anne Wilson

JUST ONE TOUCH

Harlequin Books

TORONTO • NEW YORK • LONDON
AMSTERDAM • PARIS • SYDNEY • HAMBURG
STOCKHOLM • ATHENS • TOKYO • MILAN
MADRID • WARSAW • BUDAPEST • AUCKLAND

Dedicated to the real Supermen—

Ira Kelly,
Robbie Robinson
& Jeff Smullen

ISBN 0-373-16670-2

JUST ONE TOUCH

Copyright © 1997 by Mary Anne Wilson.

Prologue

"I don't need *you* to tell me what I've done."
Mitch Rollins glared at the man blocking his exit
from his cluttered office on the third subsurface
level of Norman Tech Labs. "I know what I've
done. God help me, I know. And that's why I have
to get out of here. Now."

Luke Stewart didn't move. He gripped the sides
of the door frame, his eyes unblinking. His solid,
six-foot frame hid the view of the outer room with
the Plexiglas cages, work benches and laboratory
equipment, all of it shrouded in the dim glow of
the security lighting.

"Okay, I knew you were drunk," Luke said.
"Hell, we both were. And why not? The board
kicked you in the gut with their decision to not

permit testing on humans right now. But to come back here and—''

Mitch cut him off with a sharp motion of his hand. "Don't even go up that road, Luke. I've been there for the past twenty-four hours and it's an ugly place."

"So what did you find there?" Luke asked in a low, measured voice.

Mitch narrowed his eyes on Luke, the only person he could trust around here. The two of them had joined Norman Tech at the same time seven years ago, and Luke was as close as the brother Mitch had never had. But this time he held back, not at all sure how he could begin to explain the raw fear that had been his constant companion since he'd awakened.

"A nightmare. Something that no one can know about besides you. No one. I can't take that chance."

Luke didn't move. "It's not your choice."

"Oh, but it is my choice," he muttered to his friend, who looked disgustingly fresh in khaki slacks and a pressed white polo shirt, with his short blond hair combed back from his clean-shaven face. A distinct contrast to Mitch's rumpled jeans and dark T-shirt. He knew he had a two-day beard stubble, and his long, gray-streaked hair was tangled around his shoulders. "As far as Norman Tech goes, there's nothing. I'm off on sabbatical. They'll think I'm pouting, so let them."

Luke dropped his hands to his sides, but kept his place in the doorway. "Is it affecting your mind?"

"Not yet. I don't know if it will later on, though."

"You're thinking through a hangover, at the very least."

Despite drinking more tequila than he'd ever thought he could consume, Mitch felt better than he had in years. He'd awakened from his drunken stupor lying facedown on the floor in this room, but with no headache, no nausea, no cottony mouth. "I'm thinking clearly. Trust me. I have to get the hell out of here and protect everyone from what I've done."

"Protect? What in the—"

Mitch cut him off by reaching for the door frame, gripping the wood and, without taking his eyes off of Luke, tearing the frame away from the wall with no effort at all. "Protect," he muttered as he let the crushed wood fall from his right hand to the cement floor at his feet. "Now do you understand?"

Luke took a step back. "Oh, man." The look of horror on his face only echoed the horror in Mitch.

He gazed down at his hand, and it looked the same. It felt the same. "Now you see what I've done to myself?" he whispered.

Luke exhaled with a low whistle. "Why did you call me?"

Mitch pushed his hands into his pockets, not trusting himself to touch anything else. "I need you to cover for me here. I'm leaving." He narrowed his eyes to blur the look Luke was giving him. "If this does what I think it does, it could be devastating. Just think of the possibilities if it got into the wrong hands." That almost made him laugh, but there was no humor in the urge. "In my hands, it's bad enough. You've seen that for yourself. Now, I need your help to get me out of here without being logged out, and then I need you to keep an eye on the test subjects—monitor them, record their progress."

Luke hesitated, then finally nodded. "Okay, you've got it."

"I have a place where I can go, no questions asked, and I can work on things in peace until I get some answers. I've got enough vacation saved to take me into next year, if I need it. They'll be glad to get me out of their hair for a while around here." Mitch shrugged. "And at least I don't have anyone depending on me."

"Sad, but true," Luke said with a rueful expression.

"God, don't start that. My social life is just about the last thing I need to worry about right now." His hands clenched in his pockets. "Besides, look what

I did to that wood. If I don't concentrate every minute, it takes over and destroys what I touch.''

Luke looked down at the splintered wood, then back to Mitch. ''You might have just stumbled onto the discovery of the ages.''

''Or the curse of the ages.''

Luke silently moved back. ''Okay, let's go.''

''You take the elevator, and I'll take the stairs.'' Mitch glanced at his watch. ''I'll give you two minutes to cause a distraction at the guard station on the ground floor.''

''How are you—''

''I'll get there in time,'' he said, not about to go into the other side effects—the speed and endurance that took no toll on his body at all. No raised pulse rate, no accelerated breathing, no sweat, no exhaustion. It both fascinated him and terrified him. ''Just go.''

When Luke turned and crossed the outer lab area, Mitch flipped off the lights in his office and for an instant caught sight of himself in the huge Plexiglas cages across the lab. The image—of a lean, long-limbed man dressed in rumpled clothes—was partially blurred. Beard stubble roughened his strong jaw, and gray-streaked hair fell around his face, with its heavy brows and narrowed dark eyes.

With the shadows at his back, he looked elusive and mysterious. As he headed across the room for the stairwell, another thought formed, one that cut deeply into him. If he was right about what he thought was happening to him, he was more than elusive and mysterious. He was a monster.

Five days before Thanksgiving

HARLEY MADISON HATED the man standing less than three feet from her.

In the tiny room behind the office of a transient hotel on one of the worst streets in Los Angeles, Harley Madison faced her ugly past: Freeman Diaz.

The odors of age, decay and stale smoke mingled in the tight space, making it almost impossible for Harley to breathe. Overlaying it all was the pungency of Freeman's sickly sweet cologne. It made her stomach churn.

"You can't do this to me," she whispered, but knew how foolish those words were. Freeman could do anything he wanted to do to her. And she couldn't stop him.

"Oh, luv, I can wipe you out. You'll lose everything. No more money, no more fancy place in Malibu, no more good life. Just one more piece of white trash who came to L.A. with only her looks to sell."

Freeman came even closer. He was a slender man, barely as tall as Harley at five feet ten, with greasy hair caught in a short ponytail and a precisely trimmed goatee. His all-black attire was appropriate somehow, and he wore fake-gold rings on all but two fingers. He was part of her past, a part she thought had been buried eight years ago. But she'd been wrong. Very wrong.

He got so close that she almost choked. "And now you're mine." He actually smiled at her. "So, now that we understand each other, I'm out of here. And I'll see you the Monday after Thanksgiving, right here, midnight." He flicked her chin with one finger. "Don't be late, luv, or else…" He let his voice trail off, the implied threat stronger and more potent than words.

Harley moved abruptly, turning from him to get to the door. But as she rushed out of the office, she heard him call behind her, "You're mine, luv, all mine." Then she was outside, in the smog-laden air of the late Sunday afternoon.

No one looked at her as she hurried to her red Jeep in the parking lot. She'd deliberately dressed down to come here, in old jeans, a loose sweatshirt and tennis shoes. She'd skimmed her long ebony hair back from her face into a ponytail, hid it under a white baseball cap and forgone any makeup. No one gave her a second glance as she fumbled with the key, finally got the door unlocked and scrambled into the car.

She locked the door, then clutched the steering wheel with both hands as sickness washed over her. This couldn't be happening. Not now. Not when everything she'd ever dreamed of was within her grasp. With an annoyingly unsteady hand, she pushed the key into the ignition then took off across the parking lot with a squeal of tires.

In a painful twist of irony, right across the entrance to the motel parking lot stood a huge billboard—of Harley Madison in a bikini, drinking one of the most popular sodas in the world. She was smiling, her long dark hair ruffled by a summer breeze.

She was a woman who had caught the attention of the fashion and advertising world. A woman who didn't exist.

Harley turned the Jeep toward the freeway, not at all sure where she was going. But she wasn't going home. "I've been by your place in Malibu," Freeman had told her. "I can get to you anytime I want to." And he could. But she wasn't going to be waiting there for him.

She pressed the accelerator as she sped away from the city and Freeman's threats. The Tara Gaye Cosmetics Company wanted her for their next ad campaign. They wanted to bill her as Harley Madison, the American Dream. She swallowed a bitter sickness that rose in the back of her throat.

When her cell phone rang, she grabbed it, almost swerving into the next lane on the freeway. Quickly she turned the phone off, then opened the console to put it away. If Freeman found her home address, he could surely get her cell-phone number. But as she glanced down to put the phone away, she **saw** the gun.

She had a permit. It was for self-protection when she traveled alone. A deceptively small thing, almost toylike, it was more than enough to stop a man, the gun salesman had told her.

She dropped the phone near it, then closed the console. "The American Dream," she whispered to herself, and knew that if Freeman Diaz did what he threatened to do, her life wouldn't be a dream. It would be a nightmare.

She couldn't lose everything. Not now. Not after all she'd been through to get here. But she didn't know what to do. She had until the Monday after Thanksgiving. Time to think, to plan, to do whatever it took to stop Freeman.

Chapter One

Two days before Thanksgiving

Harley crossed the Idaho–Montana state line in the late afternoon, just as a light sprinkling of rain started to fall. She'd been driving aimlessly since leaving Los Angeles, going north, then veering east when someone recognized her near Sacramento, where she'd stopped to buy an overnight bag and some simple clothes and toiletries.

How she was recognized, she'd never know. Harley knew she'd looked awful back there, but the salesgirl had eyed her, then smiled and called her by name, as if she'd known her all her life. Harley had denied who she was, had paid with the cash she'd taken out of an ATM and had left quickly.

After that, she'd tugged her cap lower when she had to stop, kept the heavy corduroy jacket she'd bought buttoned up to her chin and made no eye contact. She veered away from cities, venturing northeastward, and finally ended up going into Montana on an all-but-deserted road that climbed into high country.

Just as the light began to fail, the rain came down heavier. Then, as it got darker and colder, the rain changed to wet snow. The Jeep took the roads well despite the growing wind and clinging snow, climbing into a land that beyond the glow of the headlights was only blurred shadows. Harley slowed a bit, hoping she'd find a town around the next bend, someplace to stop and spend the night.

But when she rounded a sharp curve, there was a flash, something quick and blurred darting right in front of the Jeep. Then it was gone, but she was already hitting the brakes. And in that split second she knew she'd done the wrong thing. There was no squeal of tires or any rubber shuddering against the pavement. The Jeep just glided as if it was floating, veering to the right into the unrelenting darkness.

Harley fought with the steering wheel and didn't even scream until she realized that there was no road to the right. There was only night and storm. Her screams echoed around her as she frantically twisted the steering wheel, but nothing stopped the Jeep from plunging off the road nose first into a bottomless void.

After a free fall through the blackness, there were ripping and crunching sounds, the feeling of rolling head over heels, of the seat belt gouging her middle and shoulders. The vehicle tumbled over and over again, totally out of control, before the end came—with a gut-wrenching jerk that sent pain through her body so sharp she couldn't define it. Then, suspended in darkness, she let a blessed nothingness claim her.

"WELCOME HOME," Mitch whispered to himself as he stepped out the back door of the clinic in Broken Junction, Montana. He didn't remember ever really having a home. His parents had died when he was three, and by the time the state had given up on finding a close relative to take him, he'd been too old to be adopted. People wanted a baby, not a six-year-old boy who wouldn't let them get near enough to figure out what he was all about. So he'd come to the Barnette Orphanage, and that had been as close to a home as he'd ever had.

"Hey, Mitch!" He heard his name being called and looked at the side of the rambling farmhouse to see an elderly man stepping carefully through the fresh snow from the storm last night. The pines and leafless trees looked stark and barren against a gray and leaden sky still heavy with more snow to come.

"Doc, I was looking for you," Mitch said.

Bundled in a red plaid jacket, jeans and heavy boots, the short, stocky man had the stride of a man much younger than his seventy years. No matter how cold the weather became, Mitch had never seen him wear a hat, even back in the years when Doc and his wife had run the orphanage. His snow-white hair was thick, and the beard that went with it was just as white—perfect for playing Santa Claus at the orphanage's yearly Christmas party.

He came to the foot of the stairs and looked up at Mitch. "I was out checking the roads at the front. It's not too bad. The truck'll take them easily when I go out on rounds."

The truck had been around as long as Mitch could remember—even back when Mrs. Barnette was alive and there were still kids here. Before the orphanage was closed down and the doctor opened the only clinic serving Crazy Junction. Actually, things hadn't changed too much. Doc was the same, just older. The rambling wooden house was the same, too. It was Mitch who had changed.

He exhaled, his breath curling into the cold air as he buttoned up his wool-lined denim jacket against the cutting chill. "You're going on rounds today?"

"I've got a few people to look in on." Doc was the last of his kind, a real old-fashioned doctor who still went on house calls and knew all of his patients and their kids by name. He'd probably delivered most of those children himself. "I can't tell you how much it means to have you back here," he murmured, cocking his head to one side to study

Mitch. "I always dreamed that one of my kids would come back and take all this over."

Mitch recoiled at the suggestion, knowing how far that was from being possible. "I told you, I'm only here for a little bit, that I'll help out in exchange for lab space and no questions. Then the lab is all yours when I leave."

"You know I can use that lab, but I just wanted you to know I was happy to see you come back...no matter why you're here."

Mitch looked around and spoke a basic truth, despite the mess he was in. "I'm glad to be back."

"Why do I get the feeling that you're waiting for something?" the older man asked softly.

Mitch closed his eyes for a long moment, then looked back at Doc. "Isn't everyone?" he asked.

"Is that a rhetorical question or a personal observation?"

"Just a thought."

Doc rubbed his hands together as he squinted up at Mitch. "And I won't ask you any more questions...for now."

"I'd appreciate that." Mitch looked out at the forest that climbed the mountains and canyons surrounding Crazy Junction. Then he came down the steps to where Doc stood in calf-deep snow. "I need to stretch my legs. I'll be back in a while."

He felt Doc touch his arm before he could walk away. "You know, Mitch, when the orphanage closed down, I thought that was it. Then my wife was gone, and the clinic just sort of happened, and took up the empty spots in my life.'' He shrugged. ''It's the lifeblood of this area now. And I'm getting old. I meant it when I asked you to consider taking over here for me.''

Mitch knew if things had been different, he might have considered the request. Being here was... He couldn't even snatch at a word that described what it had meant to drive up to the old, two-story frame house with its brick chimneys curling smoke into the gray sky. To see the trees towering around it. The barns were empty now, the tire swings long gone and a new sign, Crazy Junction Clinic, put up where the orphanage sign had been. But the rest was the same, everything from Doc to the secret paths through the woods that Mitch still remembered.

It was he who'd changed. And for the past month, he'd spent every moment he could in the laboratory he'd set up in the partial basement near the kitchen, trying to figure out just how changed he was. Doc was right: he was waiting, but he didn't know what was coming for him or when it would come. He just knew he was going to wait for it right here.

Mitch moved away from Doc and started toward the short, squat barns about a hundred yards from the house and very close to the woods. ''I'll be back in a couple of hours and get the room cleaned out for you," he said over his shoulder as he walked through the snow.

"I never saw anyone who liked being out and around more than you do," Doc called after him. "Last night you were gone for ages."

"I've got a lot of thinking to do," he said without turning. "And being out and around is therapy for me."

"I understand, after you being in that big city and all. I'll wait to go on rounds until you're here to cover for me."

Mitch stopped and looked back at Doc. One thing he didn't do unless he had to was touch things. He never touched people. He couldn't trust his own strength unless he totally concentrated on the pressure he exerted. "I told you I don't do patients, but I can do dirty work."

"Okay, you can let Stella do patients, and you can scrub floors and lock yourself in that lab you set up. Since you were in the lab most of the night, did you have a chance to run the blood sample for Dearly McCoy?"

Mitch squinted into the brightness of the cold sunlight. "Yes, it was negative. No sign of hepatitis."

"Well, that's a real relief. Did you call her?"

"No, I'll leave that up to you."

"I'll go do it, and see you when you get back."

Mitch watched him take the steps slowly. For the first time, Doc looked elderly as he made his way across the back porch and opened the door. As he went inside, Mitch turned and headed toward the dense woods beyond the old barns, walking easily through the deep snow.

Once he was past the barns and into the thick trees, well out of sight of the main house, he stopped. He took his pulse and set his watch, then with one deep breath, broke into a run on one of the old trails that led to the gorge six miles away. He never looked back.

An hour later, Mitch was on his way back, heading for a place he'd always called the edge of the world. A place he'd gone to be alone when he was a kid. A place that had taken him two hours to hike to back then. Now he'd be there in a few minutes, and back at the house a few minutes after that. He ran easily along the top of the gorge, making sure that he wasn't visible from the narrow highway less than a hundred feet away from his path.

His breathing rate was normal, his heart slow and steady, and he felt no weariness. The serum showed no signs of lessening its effects on him. If anything, he was faster than he'd been yesterday and with even more endurance. His heart was systematically beating at a lower rate, and his breathing never altered. All the tests pointed to an acceleration in the side effects, not a decline. One dose. One drunken moment. And a month later, it was working on his body with even more efficiency than when he first took it.

He ran silently, except for the crushing of snow and snapping of small branches along the way. He spotted a deer ahead of him, a female, ears pricked to the sounds, but he was past her before she had time to move. The air felt cool on his skin, the icy sunlight through the thick trees casting lacy patterns across his path. He glided, as if he were not even touching the ground. As if he were flying.

For a split second he felt something so startling that it made him stop. Right then he knew a sense of invulnerability, a flash of immortality. He stood very still, his breathing slow and steady.

Immortality? Foolish. Stupid. He was a man who had made a mistake and would have to pay for it. But invincible? Not even close. For a moment he wondered if the serum was affecting his brain, his thought processes, if he was inching toward delusions that most people read about in science-fiction books.

Then, as he started to run again, something else stopped him. This time it was a gleam of reflected light. He looked down at a piece of glass by his feet, lying on a clump of snow near the base of a huge pine tree. The sun was catching in its prisms and a rainbow of colors reflected back into the air.

Then Mitch realized there were myriad pieces

scattered in the whiteness. And the tree was gouged, limbs ripped off of it, and under the new layer of snow the ground was indented. It hadn't been this way last night when he'd run past this spot.

He turned and followed the indentations to the edge of the gorge, looked down at thick trees and snow, then at something that shouldn't have been there.

A splash of bright red mangled metal almost hidden by the trees. A glint off of chrome. A car, almost obscured from sight. He was about to run back to the clinic to call for help but then thought better of it. It would take too long, even for him, and if there was a chance someone had survived the thirty-foot plunge into the gorge, time wasn't a luxury that person could afford right now.

Carefully Mitch started down, digging in the snow as he went, half falling, then regaining his balance with the help of scrubby tress growing out of the steep side. When he finally got near the vehicle, he could see it was upside down, the force of the crash driving a good share of it into the snow and soft ground. A huge tree had been uprooted, and it had fallen across the exposed chassis.

The only visible tire was flat and torn, and the back windows were shattered, the whole frame driven in on itself by the weight of the tree. Mitch skidded down the last ten feet and grabbed at the twisted metal to steady himself. It was cold and wet from the snow. He hunkered down and tried to look through the back window, but the seats blocked his vision.

He knew there was only one way to see who was in there. He moved forward and assessed the tree trunk. It looked about two feet in diameter. He pushed one hand under it, until he'd worked his whole arm around the trunk and his shoulder and cheek were pressed to the rough bark. He maneuvered his feet until he had a strong stance, then, steadying the tree with his other hand, he concentrated and pushed.

He'd known he had superhuman strength, but he'd tested it only in the laboratory. The rest of the time he'd worked at controlling it, concentrating to ease his hold on simple objects like the handle of a coffee cup or a delicate beaker. Now he let himself go and willed the tree to move as he pulled with all his might.

Suddenly it shifted, and in one convulsive moment, Mitch lifted it and rolled it to one side. It cleared the car, crashing with a thunderous sound against another tree on the far side. There was a shuddering movement of the vehicle, shifting up and to the side, then Mitch fell backward into the wet snow.

He'd done it. The tree was gone as if it had never been there, as if it had weighed no more than a sapling. Mitch scrambled to his feet, scooting forward to the driver's side of the Jeep, and through the shattered window he finally could see that someone was in there. One person.

He could make out a woman half tangled in a seat belt, half hidden by a deflated air bag, and on her side by the twisted seat, where the console should have been. She looked like a rag doll, her limbs limp and her head down. Her dark hair veiled her face, revealing a glimpse of dark lashes against horribly pale skin. A white baseball cap was lying on the seat and what looked like a shoulder bag was tangled in the broken steering wheel. The woman wasn't moving at all, but there was no blood.

"Lady?" he called out to her. "Lady, can you hear me?"

Her eyes didn't flicker. There was no response. Mitch felt his stomach sink. He'd seen it often enough as a resident, that tinge of blue to the skin, lips faintly parted. She looked dead. He barely had time to think of how beautiful she must have been before he dropped to his knees in the snow.

He reached out as far as he could toward her, but barely touched the hollow of her throat exposed at the open neck of a corduroy jacket. With his forefinger he made contact with cold skin, and he held his breath and closed his eyes. Nothing. Then he felt a single flutter, barely discernable against the tip of his finger. Then another.

She was still alive. God knew how she could have survived the crash, but she had. He pushed in farther and heard the metal groan as his shoulder strained against it. He touched her hand, which lay limply on the seat, palm up. He felt her wrist, the delicate bones and the chilled skin, and he found it—a thready pulse. He pulled back out and suddenly realized it was snowing again, large flakes coming out of an ever-darkening sky. The temperature was dropping precariously and the cold was starting to cut through his heavy clothes.

He knew going for help was out of the question. The woman had such a flimsy grasp on life that if she had to stay here in this cold while he got someone out here, she'd be dead when they got back. He knew it for a certainty. Despite the fact that he'd never practiced medicine, going right into research, the idea of losing a life, even one he'd touched so fleetingly, was too horrible to contemplate.

He stood up and looked around, feeling the snow touch his skin with a deep chill. The woman didn't stand a chance unless he did something right away. He had to get her out of here, to where there was heat and medical help.

But pulling her out of the car the way it was would be impossible. He had to get the vehicle upright. Even with all of the strength he'd documented, he didn't know if he could move a car.

Shifting the tree had taken every ounce of strength he could muster.

He heard a soft moan and crouched to look inside. For a fleeting moment he saw blue eyes—deep, true blue. But the look in the eyes was glazed, and he knew she wasn't seeing him. "Lady, just stay still," he said, hoping she could hear him. "Believe me, you're going to be okay. I'll get you out of there."

Her eyelids fluttered, then, with a painfully weak sigh, she was gone again. Mitch moved quickly.

He trudged to the middle of the car, squatted down by the mangled metal, curled his hands around the hood where the door was jammed and braced himself. As the wind grew, driving the snow around him, he pulled with every ounce of strength he had in him and prayed it would be enough.

HARLEY WAS DYING. She knew that. She'd known it since she'd regained consciousness in the cold and dark, with her legs pinned by the dash and the steering wheel. She'd been lying almost upside down, suspended by the seat belt, which tangled at her neck and bit into her shoulders and middle. She'd managed to get her hands free and unsnap the seat belt, falling down on her side between the seats, but she hadn't been able to go any farther.

The glass was gone in all the windows. Snow and wind lashed at the car, and darkness was all around, mingling with a horrific cold. She'd tried to crawl out, but had given up. She'd found her cell phone, fallen from the open console, but there had been no signal. The gun was gone. She managed to find her purse, but nothing in it would help her now. A pen, charge cards, money, makeup—all were useless.

For hours she yelled, off and on, praying someone would hear her, but the only reply was her own voice echoing in the stormy night. And as she grew weaker and her mouth got so dry she couldn't scream anymore, she pulled her coat tightly around her and waited.

She slid in and out of consciousness, experiencing strange, undefinable dreams. Then sometime in the night she realized no one was coming. She felt colder than she'd ever been in her life, but oddly, she wasn't in any real pain. It was over. And a sadness settled into her, along with a strangely peaceful acceptance of the way things had gone.

She fumbled in her purse, found the pen, then a napkin from one of the places she'd stopped for coffee. One thing she couldn't bear was to go without saying goodbye, and barely able to see what she was doing, she managed to lay the napkin on the seat back.

"I'm so sorry," she wrote. "I never meant to hurt…" The pen fell from her fingers and she sank back into a soft blackness. She drifted into another place, far away from the horror of the stormy night. Strange thoughts flitted through her mind. The idea that she'd never have a contract with Tara Gaye Cosmetics. She'd never have to deal with Freeman, either. He was nothing now. Nothing. There was no sorrow in her. Not until one last thought skittered through her mind.

She'd never love or be loved. There'd never be a man who saw beyond the face and the body to Harley herself. There never had been, and now there never would be. She'd die alone, the way she'd felt most of her life.

The blackness was all around her, and she barely had time to grieve over what would never be when something strange happened. She'd heard about people dying and having visions in their last moments. Of tunnels of light. Of people who'd died before coming to them. But hers weren't that simple or peaceful. There were ripping, crashing sounds, and she was jolted to one side, as if she was reliving the accident all over again.

Suddenly stillness returned, but the hallucinations didn't stop. They came back to her, distorted and blurred. A voice coming down a long tunnel... Someone calling to her...

"Lady?" The voice wasn't angelic and soft, but deep and rough. She felt an odd spot of warmth at her neck, a fleeting sensation of connection, then another touch at her wrist, and the grief came again.

That sense of loss about something she couldn't define. Was it the absence of love in her life? She didn't know. But when the contact was broken, she felt horribly isolated and alone.

She heard a soft moan, then realized it was her own voice. She managed to open her eyes a bit, and there was dim light, then a shadowy blur and that voice again. "Lady, just stay still, don't move." Rough and deep, it shook her world. Real or not, it felt like an anchor to her. "Believe me, you're going to be okay. I'll get you out of there."

And she did believe.

Chapter Two

It couldn't be death. No, whatever held her was pulling her back. A lifeline preventing her from slipping further away. But Harley couldn't keep her eyes open any longer, and she sank back into a gray softness. She must have fallen deeply into hallucinations, because suddenly there were floating images that made no sense. The door of her Jeep being ripped away, metal flying. Then the voice, her anchor. "Got you," it said. "It's going to be all right."

She was being set free. She felt the weight being lifted off her and heard that voice, softly, urgently filling the spaces where horror had lived before. A man—no, Superman—doing the impossible. Then she knew how far she'd slipped into fantasy, a place where her imagination had created a safe haven for her.

She imagined someone touching her, lifting her into a cradle of warmth and safety. She was held

like a child in strong arms that radiated heat in the
painful cold that had enveloped her. Tears slipped
from her eyes when she realized what she had
imagined in her desperation. She even detected a
scent, something male and fresh.

As she moved closer to that core of heat and
safety, it was as if she was coming home. As if
she'd been looking for this place all her life. But it
didn't exist except in her mind.

The cool drops of moisture on her face weren't
real. The sense of moving wasn't real. Then she
was flying with the man, whizzing through the air,
held securely against a heart that beat steadily and
surely. She snuggled closer to that sound as air
rushed past her.

Slowly, she let go and eased back into a place of
nothingness. Her last thought was how very odd it
was to be dying and not have any fear. There was
just a sense of being where she was supposed to
be, held tightly, joined in some way to another being. She wasn't alone.

MITCH HADN'T STOPPED to figure out what moving
the car had cost him. He didn't bother with the ache
in his arms and legs. He worked at easing her out,
careful to keep her as steady as he could, then he
had her in his arms. Even through his heavy jacket
and the thick corduroy coat she was wearing, she

felt slight and delicate as he held her close to him. No heavier than a feather.

That fragility intensified his effort to make sure his hold on her stayed at a safe level. He concentrated on his grasp on her slender body as he looked up to the lip of the gorge. He couldn't take a chance of climbing out with her and jarring her, possibly hurting her worse than she already was. But he knew this land. He knew that, further down, the gorge eventually got shallow and the sides more accessible. So he pushed through the thick growth at the bottom until he found a path that had been trampled by deer and elk.

As soon as he had the clearance, Mitch took off through the snow, which was starting to fall harder. *Easy, easy,* he told himself. *Just hold her. Just carry her. And get her to the clinic for help.*

By the time he reached the place, the temperature had dropped at least twenty degrees. The wind was building, its force only partially blocked by the thick trees, which were whipped by its strength. He slowed to a jog as he got to the barns.

Smoke swirled into the sky from the chimney at either end of the building, and the world had turned gray and leaden. He crossed through the deep snow to the wraparound porch of the clinic and up to the rear entrance. He paused at the door just long enough to shift his burden, maneuver the door knob. The force of his touch sent the door crashing back against the wall, but he didn't have time to worry about that now.

He went into almost-suffocating heat in the back room and yelled, "Doc, it's me!" His voice echoed through the high-ceilinged hallway that led to the kitchen, then the front of the house. "Doc! I need help!"

He hurried through the spacious kitchen, big enough to prepare food for an army, then through a short hallway to the emergency area of the clinic. Before he could get to the arched entrance of what had once been a huge formal dining room but was now sectioned into examination alcoves, Doc was there.

In his white jacket worn over a flannel shirt and jeans and a stethoscope dangling around his neck, Doc was in the process of stripping off rubber gloves as he headed toward Mitch.

"I'm here. I'm here, so what…" His words trailed off when he saw the woman in Mitch's arms. "My God, what happened?"

"An accident," Mitch said as he moved through the archway. For the first time he realized his hands were aching from the effort to hold the woman gently, and he was thankful when he could ease her down onto the examination table.

"Quickly, tell me what you know," Doc said as Mitch stood back to let the older man get close to the woman.

"I found her in her car at the bottom of the ravine south of here." He watched the way her slender hand slid limply off the table. "I thought she was dead at first, but I got a pulse. It started snowing and the temperature dropped, so I had to get her out. Hypothermia, dehydration, probably. Maybe internal injuries. I don't know."

"Damn, I just sent Stella home." Doc checked her eyes, then lifted her hand to take her pulse. "Who is she?"

"Don't know," Mitch murmured as he watched Doc finger her fragile wrist. Out of nowhere, the thought came to him that he'd give anything to touch her like that without being terrified of hurting her. He backed up a bit more, pushing his hands into his jacket pockets. "I didn't stop to look through her things."

"I don't recognize her from around here," Doc said, studying his watch while he counted her heart rate.

Mitch knew he'd never seen her before, either. As he studied her in the stark overhead light, he knew that if he had, he would have never forgotten it.

She was maybe in her late twenties, and despite everything that was happening right now, she touched him on some level that he couldn't fathom. She had obvious beauty, with hair the color of midnight curling wildly around a delicate oval face.

The only imperfection was a slight swelling over her left eye.

Everything else about her was flawless, from perfectly arched eyebrows to elegant long lashes lying starkly against her translucent skin. Her mouth had a seductively full bottom lip, and hollows emphasized high cheekbones. But there was something more, something beyond the obvious, something that stirred him just looking at her.

The need to protect her. A gut-level need to make sure she didn't die. Mitch had never known that sense of need before, and this stranger brought it to him with a staggering impact.

As Doc undid her jacket, Mitch stared at the slight hollow at the base of her exposed throat. He willed a pulse to be there, the one he'd felt earlier, but he couldn't see a thing. "Doc, is she..."

The older man turned to Mitch, his face grim. "She's barely holding on. I just hope you found her in time," he said. "But she's hanging in there. Right now we need to get her body temp up, get fluids into her, then figure out the rest."

"Good idea."

"I'll get an IV drip going, and we need blankets," Doc continued. "I'll take care of that while you get her clothes off. They're frozen and draining away any heat she has left in her."

As Doc went to the main cabinets on the far wall, Mitch moved to the end of the table and tugged the suede boots off. When he slipped the white socks off, he could see the paleness of her feet, the tinge of blue in her nails. Quickly, he went around to the side of the table and reached for the buttons on her jacket.

The first button came off in his grasp, and he drew back to settle himself. It was unnerving to see his hands shaking, and he didn't know if the unsteadiness came from a reaction to his exertion or from his inability to see this woman as a patient.

He was taking the clothes off a stranger who looked like a sleeping angel. That last thought brought everything into focus. An angel. If he couldn't control himself and help Doc get her temperature up, that's exactly what she'd be.

Mitch moved as quickly as he could, taking off the heavy jacket she was wearing and tossing it on the floor with the boots. When he turned back to her, he made himself concentrate on mundane things. Her clothes were simple, just jeans and a white shirt. But he didn't miss the small, high breasts under the fine cotton, or the narrowness of her waist.

He was having a hell of a time shutting down his mind, especially when he reached for the snap of her jeans. But Doc rescued him. He was there with an armful of gray woolen blankets and passed Mitch half of them.

"Forget the rest of her clothes," he said.

"They're thin enough. Start wrapping her feet, while I hook up the IV. When we get her stabilized, I'll get in touch with Dumbarton and tell them we're bringing her down."

Mitch shook out the blankets and started wrapping her feet and legs, while Doc hooked up the IV on her left arm. Then Mitch stood back while he finished swaddling her like a child, until just her left arm and her face were exposed. Doc took her wrist and checked her pulse. Her hand rested limply in his, and Mitch could see the fine network of veins through the pale skin. Somewhere in his mind he noticed that she wasn't wearing any rings.

Mitch watched Doc, envying him the way he held her slender wrist in his hand. He clenched his own hands into fists behind his back. That was a loss he hadn't allowed himself to think about until he'd found this woman—that natural act of touching other people. And the bare fact was he couldn't trust himself to touch anyone anymore.

He watched Doc touch her face, finger the swelling above her eye, then move back to take her blood pressure. When he finally finished, he glanced at Mitch. "I think we got lucky. She's going to make it. No signs of frostbite or internal bleeding. She's one lucky lady, whoever she is. Lucky that you happened to find her when you did."

Mitch could feel his hands beginning to ache from clenching, and he tried to ease them open.

"Do you want me to call Dumbarton?" he asked, his voice tighter than normal.

Doc shook his head as he turned back to the woman. "I don't think so. She looks good. Her vitals are stable." He took an ear thermometer out of his pocket, then moved back the blanket to take her temperature again. When he glanced at the LED readout, he said, "It's coming up just fine, and to move her in this storm might do more harm than good. It's kicking up a hell of a fuss out there. I think it's best if we get her into a bed here, monitor her and watch for problems. Then if we need to, we can get her to Dumbarton when the storm lets up."

Mitch glanced out the small window in the high wall and could see nothing but semidarkness and driving snow. "You're probably right."

"Probably?" Doc asked with a smile as Mitch looked back at him. "So what's your suggestion?"

Mitch shrugged. "You're the doctor. It's your call."

"You found her," Doc said. "That gives you a say in this. You know about the old Chinese proverb? If you save someone's life, you're responsible for that life forever."

Mitch almost flinched at the words. The idea of being responsible for this woman was something he couldn't even begin to fathom. He shook his head sharply. "That's ridiculous," he muttered, then asked, "Where do we keep her?"

Doc frowned slightly, but let it go. "If it's my call, we'll put her in the recovery room off the kitchen."

The room had once been a huge pantry for the orphanage, but had been redone as a recovery room for patients who had had simple office procedures.

Doc tugged up the metal side rail on the bed, locked it in place, then grabbed the IV pole. "Put up the other rail, then let's get her back there."

Mitch carefully lifted the rail and locked it in place, then went around to the head of the bed. As he gripped the rail, he glanced down at the unconscious woman. An errant curl lay against the pale skin at her temple, and he reached to brush it back. But he caught himself just before his fingers touched her.

Damn it all, the longer he was near this woman, the more isolated and frustrated he felt. Doc had been right about him waiting for something, and Mitch had thought it was the time when the serum wore off. But now he wondered if this was what he'd been waiting for, this woman appearing out of nowhere. That made no sense, yet, on some level, it made all the sense in the world.

"Well, come on, son, let's get her into the back room," Doc said. "Then I'll try and get the monitor set up."

"The one you had downstairs?"

"Yes. I haven't used it for—"

"It doesn't work," Mitch said. "I tried it the other day for some...work I was doing, and the connections aren't good on it."

Doc exhaled. "Well, I guess that means I'm up all night to keep an eye on her, then. She can't be left unmonitored."

Mitch carefully measured the amount of pressure he used pushing the bed, with the doctor walking beside him, guiding the IV pole. As they moved out into the hallway toward the back of the house, Mitch said something he hadn't planned on saying. "I'll stay with her. I'm not sleepy. I've got a lot of reading to do and you've been working all day. I'll keep an eye on her."

"You wouldn't mind?"

Mitch looked down at her, at the faint flutter of a pulse at her temple, and shook his head. "No, I wouldn't mind at all."

IT WAS A LONG NIGHT of snow and wind and cold. And Mitch spent most of it in the single chair in the back room with the stranger. He tried to go through notes he'd made on his own progress, or read some journals, but nothing blocked out the presence of the woman in the bed.

He finally gave up, flipped off the overhead lights in the room, leaving on a small side light by the

bed, then went down to his room off the lab to put
the papers and books away. When he came back,
he walked into the shadowy room and stopped by
the foot of the bed. The space wasn't large, but held
a floor-to-ceiling cabinet on one wall, a sink and
the door to a half bath on the other, and the bed
and table in the middle, near the windows.

He looked down at the woman, at the IV dripping
slowly into her arm. In the low light, shadows
brushed hollows at her cheeks and throat. When he
and Doc had brought her to this room, Mitch had
excused himself on the pretext of changing out of
his snow-dampened clothes. But the truth was he
hadn't wanted to be there when Doc finally un-
dressed her and settled her in bed. Mitch didn't
think he could stand there and watch that at all.
When he'd come back, she was in the bed, in an
oversize hospital gown, and looked as if she was
sleeping peacefully.

Doc had called her a lucky woman. Indeed. If
Mitch hadn't gone out to run, if he'd stayed back
at the laboratory to do tests, he never would have
found her. No one would have found her. That
thought brought a chill that made him shiver. But
she'd be fine. Her pulse was stronger now, her temperature rising and her sleep natural...finally.

As a doctor, he should have been able to study
her objectively, in the abstract, even. But as he
stood near her, there was nothing abstract about his

thoughts and reactions. He turned from her and went to the windows to look out at the night, the wild storm and driving snow.

A soft sigh behind him startled him, and he turned, but in the soft light, he could tell she hadn't moved. Her long lashes still lay on her pale cheeks, and her hands rested on the blanket at her sides. He watched her chest under the wool blankets steadily rise and fall, reassuring evidence that things were much better for her.

He checked his watch. Midnight. She'd been back here for six or seven hours.

He carefully put his hand flat against the cold window, and knew that lust would be a given with the stranger in the bed. *Sleeping Beauty. A kiss to awaken her.* He shut that thought off, wouldn't entertain it. A delicate stranger had burst into his life and he was having misplaced feelings about being a protector. *Very* misplaced feelings.

He stood back and looked down at his hands. Hell, he couldn't even take care of himself half the time. He sure didn't need someone who depended on him in any way, shape or form.

She made another sound, and he went to the bed. Quietly he lowered the metal railing and looked down at her. Cautiously he touched the hollow at her throat and felt her pulse. Barely a contact, but it seemed so riveting to him. Her skin held warmth in it, and he had to concentrate to keep his hand still and take her pulse.

Her temperature felt near normal and her heartbeat was even and steady. He knew that she wouldn't need protecting any longer. Soon she'd be up and out of here and going back to someone who had the right to protect and love her.

He drew his hand back, breaking the contact, then leaned closer to her and spoke softly. "Lady, you're going to be fine. Just fine."

He'd barely stood back and crossed to the chair when the door opened and Doc walked in. He was in his robe, and his hair was mussed from sleep. With a passing glance at Mitch, he moved to the bed. "So you're awake. I've never seen a person who sleeps less than you, Mitch," he said. "How's our guest doing?"

"Almost normal, from what I can tell," he said as he sank into the chair.

Doc checked her out, then moved to the IV. As he started to shut it down, he spoke to Mitch. "She looks damn good. She doesn't need this anymore." He carefully took the connection out of her arm. "Has she been awake yet?"

"No, just sleeping."

"Good, she needs it. When she wakes up, find out any information you can, and we'll get through to her family. They must be sick with worry, what with this storm and her being out alone."

"Yeah, they must be," Mitch murmured as he sat forward and rested his forearms on his knees. Someone was waiting for her. Her family? A lover? Even a husband, ring or not. He had no doubt that a woman like this would have someone who cared about her and was probably scared to death that she hadn't come home.

Someone who wanted to reach out and touch her, to hold her…and protect her. He closed his eyes for a moment, squelching the thoughts this stranger stirred in him. The serum must be affecting his mind. Lust he understood; love he seldom, if ever, thought about…until now.

"It's still kicking up a mess out there," he said to distract himself. "No chance of getting to the accident site for her things. At least not for quite a while."

"I wouldn't even try." Doc reached for another chair by the wall and pulled it over near Mitch, then sat down facing him. "I appreciate you staying with her." He yawned. "I never thought I'd be saying this, but I'm getting too old for working all day, then doing this all night." He tapped Mitch's knee. "I'm getting worn out. Never thought it would happen, but it's starting."

"You'll never be old, Doc. You just keep going, like that pink rabbit."

"Now there's an image." He smiled. "Me and a pink rabbit." His smile faded slowly. "Son, I told you I wouldn't ask you any questions, and I won't. But that doesn't mean I can't make an observation, does it?''

''Could I stop you?'' Mitch asked.

He tapped Mitch's knee again, then sat back. ''Damn, you know me, don't you, son? I just wish I knew you as well.''

Mitch narrowed his eyes and rested his head on the chair back. ''You know me.''

''I don't know anything about you, except what you've told me.''

''What do you want to know?''

''For starters, when you showed up here and asked to stay, you never said if you have a family or why you wanted to come back here.''

''I have no family. My work is on hold, and I wanted to come back.''

''After twenty years, why?''

''I grew up here.''

''Mitch, do you know you're the only one who ever came back? This place, when it was an orphanage, was a place you kids wanted to get out of. You got out. You went to medical school. You became a doctor. I always thought you were bright, and that you'd make a hell of a physician.'' Doc waved one hand vaguely. ''Although you went into research instead of real doctoring.''

''I'm not good with people, not like you are.''

"You've been a big help with our Jane Doe over there."

Mitch refused to look at her. "I found her and brought her back. A plumber could have done that."

"Sure." Doc leaned forward again. "Son, you're a doctor, pure and simple, no matter what hocus-pocus you got mixed up in at that lab."

Mitch was taken aback by the man's choice of words. Hocus-pocus? He had to force himself to keep his hands open and not clench them as his muscles tensed. "Doc, don't do this to me." He knew that if things had been different, he might have thought more about what Doc really wanted from him. "I'm only staying until…" He bit back any explanation and finished with a basic truth. "Until I leave."

"Okay, no more questions." Doc held up one hand and sat back. "I won't ask where you disappear to outside for hours on end, or why you spend so much time in the lab, or why you're giving me a lab like that when you leave."

"I made a deal with you."

"Yes, and I need that lab. So I won't ask you where you got the money for it, and I definitely won't ask why you never seem to sleep." He stood. "Speaking of sleep…" He barely covered a yawn. "I'm off to bed. I've got a full day tomorrow."

"Doc, it's Thanksgiving."

"There're a couple of patients I need to check on." He glanced at the bed, then back at Mitch. "She's quite lovely, don't you think?"

"I didn't really notice."

"Sure, you didn't notice," Doc murmured, "and you got homesick for this place, too." Then he crossed the room and silently left, closing the door behind him.

Mitch sank back in the chair and closed his eyes. What he wouldn't give to be able to feel sleepy and drift off. But even that was denied him by the effects of the serum. He thought about the way the serum robbed him of time. About the periods when he blacked out, when he had no idea where he was or where he'd been.

He had no idea why the blackouts happened or when they would happen. Or worse yet, what he did while he had no memory of his actions. At least if he slept, he was under control. But he had no sleep that he didn't give himself, and he wouldn't even consider pills right now.

So he stayed there, eyes closed, trying to help his body relax, while the wind howled around the eaves of the old house and rattled the windows. He never lost that awareness of the woman in the bed, or that odd loneliness that her presence instilled in him. A loneliness he could reach out and touch, all tangled up in the darkness around him. He knew it had nothing to do with the wind and the storm or his past. It had to do with a woman he'd found in that storm, a woman who reminded him of everything he didn't have and probably never would have.

Chapter Three

Harley slowly drifted out of a soft, gentle place into a place of odd feelings and sounds. She was warm, touched by softness, but somewhere beyond the darkness there was moaning, and a rattling that echoed inside her.

For a heart-stopping moment everything came back to her: the accident and the horror of being trapped. Suddenly she felt pain, her hands and feet throbbing with a life of their own. Cautiously, she eased her eyes open, to see a high, shadowy ceiling crisscrossed with heavy beams, pale walls, shuttered windows. She caught the odors of alcohol and disinfectant.

She had no idea where she was or how she'd gotten here, or if she was just imagining the softness of the bed and the warmth in her body. Slowly she turned her head to the left and wondered if she was having more hallucinations when she saw

someone—a man who looked as if he was part of
the shadows beyond the glow of a small light.

He was sitting in a chair, his long legs thrust out
in front of him, his hands resting on his thighs and
his head against the chair back. She couldn't tell if
he was sleeping, but he wasn't moving.

Darkness on darkness. Dark clothes; a blur of
dark hair that looked overly long raked back from
a face that even touched by shadows she could tell
was strong. It was darkened even more by the
scruffy beginnings of a beard.

She wished she knew if this was real, if she was
hallucinating again or if the man was really there.
She remembered her Superman fantasies, the incredible imaginings about flying and being held.
Maybe she'd been found and was safe. Maybe her
accident had made the news. Maybe Freeman had
already done his worst. For all she knew it was all
over.

Or maybe she was still in the car and was making
up the idea of a man sitting in the shadows watching over her. A rattling and a low moaning sound
startled her, and she closed her eyes. The sounds
that had surrounded her in the car—they were still
there. But the cold was gone. Then another thought
came to her. People who were freezing to death
thought they were warm. They slipped willingly
into death, deceiving themselves about being okay.

Maybe she was dying and this was just another

illusion. Maybe this really was the madness that came with freezing to death. But if she'd wished herself here to get away from the horror of dying, why hadn't she imagined a nice place?

She almost laughed at that, but stopped when she realized that she could barely make her mouth move. Her throat was dry and painfully closed; her mouth felt as if it had been filled with cotton balls. When she tried to touch her tongue to her lips, she realized that she was thirsty and tired. Her hands and feet throbbed in agonizing pain.

If this was an hallucination, she wanted it to change. She wanted it to shift right now to something better, but it didn't. The pain and discomfort were too real. And she had the horrible feeling that Freeman would walk in at any moment to complete the misery around her.

She wasn't going to just lie here and wait. She tried to move, to get away from the pain, but couldn't. Her feet and legs were pinned. God, she really was still in the car, lost, alone, trapped by the wheel. And the horror of that thought brought a scream from deep inside her, tearing out of her parched throat and exploding in a sound of terror that echoed all around her.

Mitch had no warning. The scream came out of the shadows and rocked him, driving him to his feet before he even knew what he was doing or what was going on. Then he saw her sitting up in the bed, her hands frantically grabbing at the blankets over her legs. The screams came from her, over and over again.

He was at her side before he knew he'd moved, and almost reached out to stop her frantic flailing. But he stopped himself just before he grabbed her shoulders.

Images of the inanimate objects he'd shattered with his hands were too vivid, and he forced himself to not touch her. The fear in her was unfathomable, and whatever horror had driven the screams from her was deep in her wide blue eyes.

Every protective urge he'd fought against was back full force. He wanted to hold her, to soothe her, but he was terrified of touching her. Instead, he grabbed at the sheets and blankets she was trying to grasp and tugged them free of her legs and feet. They went flying off behind him.

"Doc, get down here!" he yelled, needing the older man to do something for her.

At the sound of his voice, she was suddenly still, her eyes on him. She looked like a deer caught in the glare of oncoming headlights. And if he'd felt protective before, the feeling almost overwhelmed him now. He sat down on the bed beside her and spoke softly. "Lady, it's all right. You're safe."

He didn't know what he expected her to do, but it wasn't for her to gasp softly and lunge at him. Before he knew what she was doing, she was burying her face in his chest and her hands were clutching his shirt. He could feel her crying, feel the heat in her, the way she was shaking, and his heart lurched painfully.

He let her hold him, a scent of light flowers from her hair invading him with each breath he took. "Lady, you're all right. You're all right. It's over."

He felt the shudder of a deep sigh run through her, then she all but melted against him. Her head nestled against his chest, and her hands slipped around him. As her silky hair tickled his chin, he forced himself to stay very still. He closed his eyes so tightly that colors exploded behind his lids, and he knew a pain that had nothing to do with physical discomfort.

He ached in his soul and knew there was nothing he could do to stop it, just as he knew he couldn't hold her. But for that moment, he let himself sense her against him, as delicate as anything he'd ever experienced in his life. And he was stunned by the idea that if things had been very different, he could hold this woman forever.

Harley heard the voice. It cut through everything—the panic, the fear. It was the same voice she'd heard before, shouting something. Then she saw him, standing over her as the linen disappeared somewhere behind him.

He was tall, lean and dark. And he looked for all

the world like a safe harbor to her. A place she could go and know that things would be all right.

Lady, it's all right. You're safe.

The voice rumbled through her, rough and deep, and comforting in a way that defied description. In that moment, Harley didn't care if this was all a product of her neediness or not. She shuddered and let go, leaning into a strength that felt familiar and right. It was as if that contact took the weight of the world off her shoulders.

Tears silently slipped down her cheeks and she closed her eyes tightly as she grasped the soft cotton of his shirt in her sore hands. He felt like a rock, for her to lean against, solid and sure. If this was an hallucination, so be it.

You're all right. It's over.

It *was* over, and with a deep sigh, she settled against him, slipping her arms around his waist. She felt a heart beating against her cheek and had a flashing memory of a heart beating close to her before, in her fantasies. But gradually, she grasped the fact that this was real. Very real.

She could feel each breath he took, each heartbeat that thumped in his chest. She inhaled a mixture of heat, soap, water and something she could only call maleness. And gradually that easing in her began to shift into something else. Something less safe. Something that made her draw back, needing to know what this reality actually looked like.

As she opened her eyes, she found reality right in front of her. She was looking into the face of the man who had been in the chair before. He was so close she heard each rough breath he took. So close that, in the low light and through the remnants of tears, she could see harshly etched features. A strong jaw, scruffy with the beginnings of a new beard; a sharp nose that had seen the wrong end of a punch or two; heavy brows slashed above hazel eyes that were narrowed on her right now. He wasn't touching her, yet she felt as if she was caught in some web of his making, a place that joined her to him in an invisible way that was more disturbing than anything she'd experienced with a man before.

And it was real. So real that all she had to do was to reach out and touch him. But when she would have made that connection, she felt pain in her hands, a throbbing overlaid with a prickling fire. When she looked down at them, lying on the stark white gown she had on, she flinched at the sight, they were so red and swollen.

"My...hands," she said, her voice a rasping whisper. She lifted them palms up to look at them more closely.

"Your circulation's coming back, and it's going to be uncomfortable, but there's no permanent damage."

She stared at her hands, then slowly lowered

them to her sides. It was then she realized her clothes were gone, and all she had on was a very short hospital gown. "Oh," she croaked.

"Just a minute," the man said, and when she looked up at him, there was an uncontrollable image of him undressing her while she'd been unconscious.

She was certain the thought would be written on her face and was thankful he wasn't looking at her. He was reaching to one side, then turned to offer her a drink from a white glass with a straw in it.

He held it close enough for her to take a sip from the straw, and murmured, "Drink, but do it slowly. We can talk when you get some liquids into you."

The cool water trickled into her mouth, but despite the fact that it felt wonderful, she could barely swallow. When she finally managed to get some down, she could feel her throat starting to free up. She took another drink, aware of his hand holding the glass for her.

When he put it on the side table, Harley moved back and leaned against the metal headboard of the bed. She glanced down at her hands again, finding the fiery redness unsettling. Almost as unsettling as all the unanswered questions bombarding her at the moment.

He must have seen her looking at her hands, because she heard him say, "Don't worry. You're going to be just fine. Trust me. I'm a doctor."

She glanced up at him. A doctor? He didn't look like any doctor she'd ever seen before. He actually didn't look like any man she'd known before. She'd never been studied by narrowed eyes like that, and she suddenly realized those hazel eyes didn't have that touch of recognition in them she'd come to expect from any man who looked at her.

"Your feet are going to be a bit uncomfortable, too, but they were more protected than your hands."

He was acting as if he didn't know who she was, as if he'd never seen her before. Could he be the only person in the country who hadn't seen a billboard or a magazine ad?

"Can you talk a bit?" he asked in that deep voice that seemed to vibrate the air around her.

"A bit," she managed to reply.

He stood, but didn't move away from the bed. Instead, he towered over her, his eyes dark and unreadable in the dim light as he said, "Now that you're awake, you can tell us who you are and who to contact."

He didn't know who she was. A part of her relaxed just a bit. Maybe there wouldn't be any need for anyone to know about this. But there had to be other people around. She couldn't be here with just this man. She tensed again at that thought and ignored his question to ask her own. "Where...am I?"

"The Crazy Junction Clinic."

She'd never heard of it. "Where?"

"Montana. We're tiny, but the clinic's the best. You're in good hands. Trust me."

She met the scrutiny of his hazel eyes. "How...how did I get here?"

"You were found at the accident site, just south of town."

As she looked up at the doctor, the visions of someone ripping off the door of the Jeep, of carrying her forever, flashed through her mind. She touched her tongue to her cold lips. "Accident?"

He studied her for a long moment. "Do you remember what happened?"

She took a shaky breath and closed her eyes, but she opened them immediately when she saw strange things behind her lids. A light; shredded metal flying... "I—I don't," she whispered.

"That happens. Blanking out the actual accident."

She realized that her hands and feet were still aching, but not nearly as badly as they had at the first. She uncurled her fingers and lifted them. "What happened to my hands?"

"Hypothermia. It got pretty cold out there, and I didn't know how long you'd been trapped."

He turned abruptly and opened the door. "Doc!" he called out. "Can you come down here?" When a muffled voice echoed back to him, he returned to the bed, leaving the door slightly ajar.

He reached to one side and produced a thermometer. "Let's just check you out and make sure you're doing as well as it looks like you are."

He put the thermometer in her mouth, then moved back a bit. Since he'd said he was a doctor, she expected him to take her pulse or feel for a fever, but he didn't touch her. He merely studied her intently, with eyes that made nervousness tighten her neck and shoulders.

She had no idea how long she'd been in the wreck or how long she'd been at this place, either. Then her heart lurched. She'd been worried about him recognizing her, of the press being drawn here for the story, of Freeman finding out where she'd gone. But something else hit her. She could have been trapped for days in the Jeep. She could have lost all sorts of time. She could have missed the deadline Freeman had given her.

She tried to take the thermometer out of her mouth, but her fingers wouldn't work and the glass tube fell to her lap. "What day is it?" she whispered.

"Wednesday." He bent down and picked up the thermometer, brushing her bare thigh in the process.

She started slightly at the contact, her eyes flying to his, but he seemed lost in concentration as he put the thermometer very carefully back in her mouth.

"What Wednesday?" she asked in a muffled voice around the thermometer.

"The Wednesday before Thanksgiving."

She sank back weakly. Everything was still ahead of her. The Tara Gaye contract offer—and Freeman. She shivered slightly at the thought of the man, but the doctor moved back, grabbed the sheets and blankets off the floor.

He shook them out, making the material snap sharply in the air before it billowed down around her bare legs. He muttered an oath under his breath as he moved back, not touching the linens again as they settled over her.

He met her gaze and murmured, "Sorry, I'm— I'm not good at making beds." He reached for the thermometer, studied the slim glass tube with intense scrutiny, then looked at her with those hazel eyes. "Nearly normal. You've very lucky."

Wind howled outside and she heard the glass in the windows rattle. One look at the dark panes and she could tell the storm she remembered was still raging. At least she'd been lucky this time.

"When did you have the accident?" the doctor was asking.

She bit her lip hard. "I...I don't remember."

He moved a little closer. "Do you remember what caused it?"

She recalled the flash in front of her, something darting across the road. "No," she whispered.

"It's okay. It doesn't matter right now. All that counts is that you're going to be fine."

She wished that was true. "Doctor—?"

"Call me Mitch. I don't answer to 'doctor' very often," he said. "And what do we call you?"

She stared up at him and knew if she said her name, it could give her away completely. How many women were called Harley? It was a coolly fashionable name now, but when she'd first gotten the nickname it was because she'd liked to ride on the back of her father's motorcycle. And Hannah, her given name, didn't exist anymore.

No, she couldn't tell him her real name. She'd been lucky enough to find one person who didn't recognize her, and she needed time to think about what to do now.

"You don't remember your name?"

She swallowed around the tightness in her throat and found herself shaking her head to buy time. "I don't—I don't know."

He was closer again, sitting on the edge of the bed, bringing himself to eye level with her. She could barely meet his gaze. She'd never been good at lying, and she was definitely uncomfortable lying to this man. "You don't remember who you are?"

He gave her the answer that would buy her time she needed for now. "I don't think so."

He raked his fingers through his hair. "It's not unusual for accident victims to have partial amnesia for a short period of time after trauma,'' he said. ''But there's nothing? No name at all?''

Why was lying to this man so distasteful? She swallowed hard and murmured, ''I—I don't think so.''

A door opened, then another man was there—an older, stockier man with short gray hair, wearing a faded blue bathrobe. ''Mitch, what's going on?''

He came over to the bed and looked down at Harley. ''Ah, so our guest is finally awake.'' He had a soft, comforting voice that matched the expression on his face. ''I'm Dr. Barnette. Everyone calls me Doc, and I'd say you're one lucky girl. If Mitch hadn't found you out there...'' He shook his head and the smile faltered a bit. ''Well, the storm was pretty bad last night, and not much better tonight.''

She darted a look at Mitch, who was watching her narrowly. The man had a way of looking at her as if she were a bug under a microscope. But the effect on her hadn't anything to do with clinical observations. The man made her uneasy with just a look, and she backed away from asking herself why that was so. ''It sounds terrible,'' she whispered.

''It's bad enough.'' He looked at Mitch. ''How're her vitals?''

Mitch moved back a bit. ''Her temperature's up to normal.''

''Great, that's a relief. Anything else?''

"I was waiting for you."

"Well, let's see what we have going on here," he said as he reached for her hand, and he kept talking as he methodically checked her out. Finally, as he held her wrist and stared at his watch, he said, "So, who are we having to Thanksgiving dinner?"

"She can't remember much," Mitch said, moving back even more to where the shadows of the room blurred his features. "A touch of trauma-induced amnesia."

Doc checked her eyes. "So, you don't have a name?"

"I—I must," she said.

"So you must, but what are we to call you?" He looked down at her. "It's your choice, until your memory comes back or until Mitch can reach your car to get your things out of there."

She hadn't thought of her purse and papers in the car. Or the gun. She touched her tongue to her lips. "I don't care."

He shook his head. "I always hated the Jane Doe tag. Sounds like a deer to me."

"I—I guess it does," she said, a smile almost coming at his words. But her lips were tight and vaguely sore. And she remembered that horrible thirst when she was trapped, and again when she'd awakened here. "My car—is it really badly damaged?" A silly question, when she remembered it lying on its top. No, it had been turned over by the man in her visions. But that didn't make any sense. Maybe it had never rolled over at all. Maybe it was drivable. But that slim hope was dashed by the doctor.

"Well, from what Mitch tells me, it's beyond repair."

No car. She'd have to figure out how to get back to L.A. by Monday. But for now, she didn't want any part of that city or what was waiting for her there. "What a mess," she whispered, her voice vaguely shaky.

"Hey, but you're all right. Things aren't too bad, are they?"

"No, not too bad," she said, knowing what a lie those words were. Her whole life was hanging in the balance.

Doc smiled again. "And you're going to get a great Thanksgiving dinner out of all of this. So all is not lost." He glanced at Mitch. "I'm going to get her something to help her relax." With a gentle pat on Harley's hand, he said, "Everything's going to be just fine." Then he hurried out of the room.

Harley looked at Mitch, still standing in the partial shadows, and slowly rubbed her sore hand where the doctor had touched her. "Why didn't you tell me you were the one who found me?"

"It didn't come up." He nodded at her hands. "How bad's the pain?"

The burning was easing and any aches were general. "Not too bad now."

As he moved closer to the bed, he raked his fingers through his hair. Gray streaked the dark locks that waved slightly where they fell from a central part to his shoulders. "And your throat?"

She swallowed and knew that the tightness there had little to do with her ordeal. It seemed more and more to be a product of him coming closer, so close she had to tilt her head to peer up at him. He look rough-hewn, not at all what she supposed a real doctor would look like. "Are you really a doctor?" she asked before she had time to edit her words.

His hazel eyes narrowed on her. "I'm a real, honest-to-God doctor. But I don't practice."

She was beginning to recognize that way he had of squinting at her with his head slightly cocked to one side when he was studying her. It made her wish Doc was here, a gentle man who was comforting, instead of a man who... She couldn't come up with a word for Mitch. *Edgy? Unsettling? Disturbing?* None of them were just right, and she didn't know what the right word would be. Until it came suddenly and clearly to her. *Sexy.* The man exuded a male sexuality that almost took her breath away.

Chapter Four

"Why...why don't you practice?" Harley asked, to blunt the power of the thoughts running through her mind.

He shrugged and tucked his hands in the pockets of his pants. "Let's just say I went in other directions. I found things that seemed more important than day-to-day medicine."

"I can't imagine what could be more important than saving people's lives," she murmured.

"Lady, I can tell you it sure isn't a regular occurrence to come across someone in the woods." His lips lifted in the shadow of a smile, and for a moment Harley felt herself tensing, waiting for the full expression. But at the last minute, he glanced away from her to the windows. "And this storm is unusual for this time of year, too. A world of surprises," he said softly, then turned back as the door opened and Doc came into the room.

The smile was completely gone, leaving his face

dark and his expression unreadable as he watched the older man approach the bed.

Doc held out two tiny pills to Harley. "Take these and you'll sleep. That's the best thing for you now." She was saved from having to move her fingers when Doc held the tiny pills to her lips. She got them on her tongue, then he offered her the white glass Mitch had earlier. The pills slipped down with the cool water, then Harley sat back.

"That'll make you feel sleepy in a bit. Don't fight it."

"I don't know how to thank you for all you're doing for me."

He waved that aside with one hand. "Just get some rest. We'll talk in the morning. Maybe when you wake up, you'll remember everything. I just hate to think someone's worried sick about you not showing up at home or not calling when you promised to."

The lie lay bitter on her tongue, but she was in too deep to suddenly "remember" everything. "Maybe so," she said, cringing a bit when the windows rattled from a particularly hard blast of wind.

"Don't worry. This old house has survived worse than this. Mitch can tell you all about the great storm around twenty-five years ago. Snow so deep it covered all the windows on the ground floor." Doc looked at Mitch with a smile. "Come to think of it, I think that's the year you and two other boys made a makeshift sled out of the ironing board, went out the window of the dormitory and sank into ten feet of snow.''

"An ironing board?" she asked.

Mitch shrugged. "It seemed like a good idea at the time, but it didn't work."

"Experimenting even then," Doc murmured. "A boy with ideas, some very ingenious ones."

Mitch glanced at the windows. "Some stupid ones, too," he muttered tightly, and Harley had no idea where that flicker of anger in his voice came from.

Doc looked at him hard for a moment, then turned to Harley, his face softening. "Everything will be better in the morning."

Harley certainly knew enough about stupid ideas, and she couldn't hold back a deep sigh. "I hope so."

"Listen, you survived without any permanent damage, and even an old country doctor like me can tell you that amnesia can be transitory. You just need time for your mind to catch up with things." He suddenly chuckled. "Although the last time I thought I had an amnesia case, it was Willis Holland trying to put one over on his wife. The guy disappeared overnight and tried to get Vera to believe he forgot where he'd been. A perfect story, if he could have made it work. But Vera wasn't exactly the trusting sort. They'd been married thirty years. The woman got wise to him.''

Harley found herself almost smiling. ''So she didn't believe him?''

''Oh, she let him believe that she did,'' Doc said with a sly smile. ''Then she got her shotgun and tracked down the girlfriend.''

Mitch watched the woman in the bed listening to Doc, and when the punch line came, he saw her eyes gleam with laughter, then her pale lips manage to curl weakly at the corners. ''You—you don't mean it,'' she whispered, her voice still a bit hoarse, but getting better all the time.

He took a step back as the impact of her expression reverberated through him. He'd seen beautiful women before—more than he remembered now— but he couldn't recall one who claimed his attention so fully. No makeup, hair unbrushed, a poorly fitting hospital gown…even so, something about her drew him like a moth to a flame. And the concept of ''stupid mistakes'' took on a whole new meaning.

''Oh, I mean it,'' Doc was saying. ''Of course, the gun never was fired, just used for threatening, but Vera ended up in jail overnight for the stunt. Willis was such a good husband after that.''

When the patient chuckled softly, the overly large hospital gown slipped off one slender shoulder. Mitch barely covered a gasp when he saw the bruises on her pale skin. One was at her neck, where the seat belt must have cut into her at impact, but the other bruises didn't come from the accident at all. They were dark purple marks, four of them—bruises that he knew would match his fingers, where he'd held her to carry her here.

He barely repressed the nausea that rose in his throat and pushed his hands behind his back. God help him, he'd thought he'd been careful holding her when he was running. But he hadn't been careful enough.

"Are you hungry?" Doc was asking her.

She looked a bit taken aback by the question, but nodded in surprise. "You know, I think I am."

Doc smiled at that. "Well, that *is* a good sign. We'll see what we can rustle up in the kitchen."

"You—you don't have to bother the cook."

Mitch moved away from the bed toward the door, unable to glance at her.

"You're looking at the cook," Doc said. "This is a very small facility, and we seldom have anyone staying overnight, but I think I could manage some soup for you."

"I don't want to put you out."

Mitch was at the door, and turned just before he walked out. He caught a flashing glimpse of Doc tugging the shoulder of the gown back over her, and he turned from the sight. "I'll get the soup," he said, and left quickly, closing the door behind him before Doc could stop him.

He stood in the hallway outside the door, trying to take an even breath, then looked down at his hands. They were shaking, reflecting his own horror at what he'd done to her. He hated what his hands could do without him even thinking about it, when he was only doing what normal people did. He clenched his fingers into fists, and barely stopped the urge to hit the wall as hard as he could.

When he heard soft laughter behind the door, he hurried away from the sound to the kitchen. No matter what he thought when he looked at the woman in the bed, he had no right to even wonder what it would be like to touch her. He'd touched her once and left his mark. He wouldn't hurt her or anyone again.

WHEN HE CAME BACK into the room, carefully carrying a tray with the soup on it, he stopped just inside the door. The woman was very still, lying back, supported by extra pillows that kept her in a half-sitting position. Her eyes were closed, and Doc was nowhere in sight.

Mitch crossed to the bed and looked down at her. Her color was better, and her hands, resting loosely on the blanket, looked less red and swollen. He cleared his throat, then saw the long, dark lashes flutter before they swept up, and he was looking into those incredible blue eyes.

"Your soup," he murmured as he set the tray on the movable side table, then swung it over the bed. He concentrated as he tugged it into position in front of her, then moved the soup and spoon closer. "All we had was chicken soup," he said, needing to talk to fill the spaces that seemed so charged when he was around her.

"Chicken soup," she whispered, and her voice was softer and smoother. He wasn't sure if that was good, when it made him even more aware of her. "That sounds like something a doctor would prescribe."

He looked at her and wished he hadn't. She was smiling now, a real smile that curved her lips and touched the deep blue depths of her eyes. The expression totally disarmed him, and he found himself stammering something about the old remedies being the best.

He looked away from her as she sat up, and he was startled when she muttered, "Damn it all, anyway."

When he looked back at her, she was fumbling with the spoon, but she couldn't hold it with her slightly swollen fingers. The spoon clattered to the tray, barely missing falling into the soup. "I—I can't seem to hold the damn thing. My fingers won't cooperate at all."

He looked back toward the door. "Where did Doc go?"

"He said since I was in good hands, he was going to get some sleep." She touched the spoon with her finger, nudging it in his direction. "I hate to ask you this, but could you feed me some soup? I'm really hungry."

Mitch didn't have any idea how to refuse to help her, so he sank down on the edge of the bed and very deliberately reached for the spoon and picked it up. If he kept his focus on his grip, he was okay. He knew that. Carefully, he dipped the spoon in the warm soup, then lifted it to her lips. *Just do it*, he told himself. *Just do it.*

She sipped the liquid from the spoon, then, as he scooped another spoonful, said softly, "I feel so embarrassed to be this helpless. I haven't had anyone feed me since I was..."

Harley's words trailed off when she realized she'd been about to say since she was six and had the measles. When Mitch looked at her expectantly, she shrugged. "I can't remember, but it must have been a long time ago. I'm sorry."

"Lady, don't apologize," he murmured. "Just eat."

"I sure won't ask you to do the airplane trick," she whispered, needing to feel a lessening of the tension that had come into the room with Mitch's return.

The spoon stilled in the bowl as he looked back at her. "Excuse me?"

"You know—when you were a kid and your mother wanted to get you to eat, she pretended that the spoon was an airplane and it was coming in for a landing in the hangar?"

"No, I didn't know," he muttered, holding the spoon to her mouth again. "You remember that?"

She sipped more of the liquid, backtracking as she said, "No...I thought every kid had that done to them." She was a lousy liar. "I think I did."

He stirred the soup without looking at her, clicking the spoon on the sides of the bowl. "Maybe kids who had what passes for normal lives did, but I wouldn't know about that."

"Oh," she whispered, and even though she thought she'd been ravenous, her appetite was gone abruptly, chased away by the tinge of pain in his eyes. She swallowed, then sank back in the pillows. "I'm sorry."

"I told you to stop apologizing." He glanced around the room. "This place used to be an orphanage, and I was one of the orphans. We didn't have much time for games at dinnertime. You ate and ate fast, or you missed out."

His words sounded flat and unemotional, and that bothered her on some level she didn't understand. She was almost ready to say she was sorry again, but one look from those hazel eyes as he squinted at her and she knew that the last thing this man wanted was sympathy. "So—so you grew up here?" she asked, just to say something. "And you tried to ride an ironing board out of the second-floor window?"

"I'm surprised Doc remembers that little incident." Mitch started stirring the soup slowly. "I'd forgotten all about it, until he brought it up. A past better forgotten," he muttered as he lifted the spoon to her again.

A past better forgotten. Her past. She sipped the warm liquid, then sank back in the pillows Doc had pushed behind her earlier, a distinct feeling of weakness invading her. "People never forget," she whispered, but the memory of Freeman seemed to be receding just a bit. She could feel a blurring in her mind, as if every hard edge of life was being dulled. "You wish they would," she murmured, her tongue beginning to feel thick. "But they don't. And every stupid mistake you make comes back to haunt you."

"The price of stupidity," Mitch said. He drew back from her, receding into the blur of shadows as he swung the tray away from the bed and stood over her.

The price of stupidity? Harley could have almost laughed at that as she sank lower in the bed. What price would she have to pay? "It gets pretty expensive sometimes, doesn't it?" She sighed.

"It's too late for this discussion," Mitch was saying from somewhere above her. "Way too late."

Nothing mattered now, not even Freeman, as the softness around Harley cushioned everything. "Yes, too late," she whispered.

"Sleepy?" Mitch was asking, his voice low and vaguely muffled.

"Sleepy," she echoed softly.

"Any idea who's sleepy?" he asked.

She looked up at him. He was close to her, lifting up a side rail, then holding the metal and bending over her, looking at her intently. Whatever Doc had given her was making her less tense about his closeness, letting her absorb his dark features without all the nervous edginess this man brought with him.

"Do you remember anything yet?" he asked.

The drug was taking effect quickly, and any defenses she had were systematically lowering. "I remember your voice," she admitted, her tongue starting to be a bit uncooperative.

"What?"

"Your voice—I remember that. You—you talked to me.... I remember."

"What else do you remember?" he asked.

Her eyelids fluttered, threatening to close, but she could see him, a shadow over her. "Being alone. Then...you...saved me. You—you..." She managed to lift her left hand and touched his where it gripped the rail. "Thank you...for saving me."

Her strength was gone, and the sense of contact with Mitch was fleeting before her hand slid weakly down to the blankets. She saw him watching her, then saw a look of shock on his face as he looked down at his hands. It was then she noticed something that wasn't possible.

Mitch was pulling his hands back, and the metal of the rail was twisted and distorted. It had been straight and smooth, but now...

She couldn't keep her eyes open, and before she could even try and figure out what was going on, sleep pulled her into dark softness. The last thing she thought she heard was Mitch whispering, "My God."

Mitch stared down at the rail, at the way his hands had lifted it into a twisted arch as if it had been soft plastic. God, he couldn't even remember doing it. All he remembered was her touching him—her hand on his, her fingers light against his skin—and the way his body responded to that simple contact.

Then he looked down at her, thankful that she had fallen asleep. She wouldn't see this, and there wouldn't have to be any explanations. Carefully, he touched the metal again, easing his fingers along it, pressing until it was as close to its original shape as possible. Then he drew back.

If he looked closely, he could make out slight ridges, but if a person didn't know better, it looked normal. He pushed his hands behind his back before he glanced at her again. Then he wished he hadn't. She breathed a soft sigh that ran riot over his frayed nerves as she shifted to one side. The action tugged at the gown, exposing her slender shoulder again.

Sickness rose in Mitch's throat at the sight of the even-darker bruises, and he turned from the bed. He almost ran into the swinging tray with the soup on it, but sidestepped it and quickly left the room. With his hands gripped into tight fists at his side, he went past the kitchen and hurried down the steps to the half basement, where he'd put the lab together.

He needed space, time to regroup. Time to think about stupid mistakes in his past that were costing him more and more all the time.

Mitch spent the rest of the night in the lab, but checked on the woman every hour. He never went any closer than the foot of the bed and he never touched her or anything else in the room. He just looked at her, checked to make sure her breathing was easy and her coloring good, then he left.

When dawn came, the storm had let up. Mitch showered, dressed in jeans, a flannel shirt and his heavy coat and boots, then left a note for Doc, saying that he was going to get the woman's things out of the wreckage if he could. After fastening the message to Doc's office door, he went through the reception area, which used to be the formal living room, and out the front door.

He stepped onto the wraparound front porch into air so cold it almost burned to breathe it. Snow was still falling, but it was light and soft. Mitch stood for a moment scanning the all-but-buried driveway, which curved up from the open metal gates down by the road. Then he tugged on his navy wool watch cap and went down the steps into knee-deep snow.

He needed to move, to put some distance between himself and this place for a while. His boots crunched in snow that would have slowed a normal man, but he made his way easily around the house. Then he cut toward the barn and the woods. Once he was out of sight of the clinic and among the dense trees, he set off at a dead run.

He cut through the silent, snow-burdened forest, heading for the gorge and the wreck to find out just who the woman in the clinic was. He made it to the accident site at the bottom of the gorge just as the sun crested the edge of the gorge. And the last thing he remembered was seeing that the car had been buried completely in the newly driven snow.

THE CAR WAS out of control, rolling and pitching into darkness that held a horror Harley couldn't see but she knew was waiting for her. It never came, however. She was being held, pulled into warmth and comfort, then flying into a blue sky where air shimmered and the sun danced all around. Arms supported her, hands touched her. A voice filtered into her, deep into her soul—a voice she reached for and held to her. Comfort and sureness. A total lack of fear.

Then everything was gone. Everything was denied her. Suddenly it was Freeman's voice whispering in her ear, telling her horrible, ugly things, shutting out all the good and replacing it with repulsive images. She fought to get away from him, running, falling. She saw Mitch in front of her and reached out to him. But he didn't move. He just watched her, his hands out of sight behind his back.

All she wanted was for him to take her hands, to hold her to him, to feel his reality, a reality that could chase away all the grotesqueness that Freeman brought with him. But there was nothing. No words, no touch, no anchor for her.

She woke suddenly with a violent start. She was shaking and her face was wet with tears. She stared above her at the high ceiling, at cool gray light that filtered into the room. And she was alone. Completely alone.

Damn dreams. She'd never been one to have them before, but she felt as if she'd been pummeled by them now. A feeling of loss and frustration ate at her, and she tried to breathe evenly and slowly.

She wanted to settle the world for just a moment so she could think and orient herself.

As the tightness in her began to ease, she exhaled in a rush, then realized that any pain she felt wasn't physical. She lifted her hands, turning them back and forth in front of her. They weren't aching anymore and looked almost normal. Hands... Why did that bring a thought to her that she couldn't quite grasp? She lowered them, then eased herself up to a sitting position and looked around the room.

No one was there. Mitch and Doc were gone, and the silence was complete. She was glad to be alone for a few minutes to collect herself. She pushed at her tangled hair to get it off her face, then tucked it behind her ears and realized that she had to go to the bathroom.

She reached for the rail that blocked her from getting out of bed, and suddenly had a strange memory come to her. Or was it a dream? Whatever it was, it was only a flashing glimpse of Mitch bending metal.

She touched the cold rail with her fingertips, but it felt straight and smooth. It was only a stupid dream, part of a nightmare that made no sense, no more than flying had made sense. But as she gripped the metal support to lower it, she felt almost indiscernible ridges in the hard metal.

She ran her fingers over them. They were definitely there, but they couldn't have been from anything Mitch had done. They had to be imperfections in the manufacturing. She lowered the rail and swung her legs over the side. For a moment she caught sight of bruises on her thighs—a large one just above her knee, and in the middle of her outer thigh, wrapping around it, four straight bruises, each about two inches long. A reminder of being pinned by the seat and the steering wheel.

She looked away quickly and slipped out of the bed, holding the headboard for support. For a moment she had no balance and gripped the metal tightly to keep from falling, then the world began to settle, and she could stand on the cold wooden floor. She took another moment to grow steady, then looked around and saw a door near the side of the bed.

Carefully, she walked barefoot in the skimpy gown to the door, opened it and found a small bathroom with a freestanding sink, a toilet, tiny shower stall. One high window was almost blocked by frost etching the glass. She used the toilet, then went to the sink and ran cool water over her hands.

When she glanced at the mirror above the sink, she understood why Mitch and Doc hadn't acted as if they had ever seen her before. She had a slight discoloration and swelling above her left eye, her skin was pale, the freckles standing out vividly, and her hair was a wild tangle around her shoulders.

She looked away, ran more cool water over her hands, then pressed her hands to her face.

When she stepped out of the bathroom, she felt a bit better, and knew she had to leave the clinic as soon as she could get a car. She couldn't take the chance of finally being recognized, and a part of her just didn't want to lie to Mitch and Doc anymore. It was distasteful to her and made her horribly uneasy, especially after everything they'd done for her. But blurting the truth was out of the question.

She stood on the cool floor and looked around for her clothes, but didn't see them. Crossing to a huge cabinet on the opposite wall from the bathroom, she opened it, but found it stocked with linens and medical supplies.

Just as she shut the cabinet, the door to the room opened and she turned, expecting to see Mitch or Doc, but neither one was there. A tiny woman dressed all in white walked in, carrying a tray with a pitcher and glasses on it. She looked at the bed, then glanced to her left, saw Harley, and her eyes widened.

"Oh, my gosh," she breathed, and Harley knew that someone had finally recognized her.

Chapter Five

Harley braced herself, ready to beg the woman to keep her secret if she had to. Then she realized that the woman didn't recognize her at all. She suddenly smiled, then motioned to the bed. "My dear, you are not suppose to be up. Doc'll have my head for letting you wander around like this."

Harley stood where she was.

"It's wonderful that you're awake and all, don't get me wrong," the woman continued, putting the tray on the side table, then hurrying over to Harley. "You're looking pretty chipper considering everything you've gone through." She barely came to Harley's shoulder, but that didn't stop her from taking her by the arm and leading her back to the bed. "But you really can't be up yet. Doc told me what you've been through. He's sure not expecting you to be making a tour of this place."

Harley sank down on the side of the bed, but

didn't get back in it. "I actually feel okay," she said.

The woman put her hands on her hips. "Well, I just think it's a miracle that Mitch found you like that. I mean, you could have been there forever and no one would have seen you, but Mitch, he roams all over the woods." She moved to the table and poured a glass of water while she kept talking. "That boy goes out at dawn and doesn't come back for hours." She turned and offered Harley the glass. "Here, you need to get fluids back in you. Drink up."

While Harley took the glass, cradling it carefully in both her hands and slowly sipping the cool liquid, the woman chatted on. "Now, you just tell me what you need and I'm here to do whatever you want. That's my job. That's why Doc pays me all those big bucks." She laughed suddenly, a bark of humor at her own joke. "That's me, the wealthy one. Now, tell me what you need."

"I—I don't mean to put everyone out."

"Oh, dear, forget that stuff. Doc's just happy to have people around. I mean, when Mitch showed up out of the blue a month back, you would have thought it was Christmas. Doc just perked right up. He's older, you know, and he's still a good doctor, but he'll be needing someone to take over for him. After all the kids he helped give a chance to, you'd have thought some of them would have come back here. But no, just Mitch. Out of the blue. Just showed up.''

She went around the bed, talking all the while as she smoothed the sheets and blankets. She fluffed the pillows against the headboard, then came around and urged Harley to sit back into the pillows. It was easier just going along with the little dynamo, so Harley leaned back and rested her feet on the smoothed blanket.

"That Mitch, all grown up. But I remember when he was just a boy, full of mischief. He led Doc and the missus on a merry ride at times, I'll tell you that. First he was real shy and solemn, but he came out of that so nicely. And he was real bright. Doc always knew that he was special.''

Harley didn't have a chance to say anything as the woman popped a thermometer into her mouth, then started to take her blood pressure. "Anyone looking at him could tell he was special. Then he came back.'' She straightened and read the thermometer. "Always knew he would. I just wish…'' She shook the mercury down, then looked at Harley. "Well, you seem just fine to me, but I'm no doctor. Just a nurse.''

"What do you wish?'' Harley asked.

"Excuse me, dear?''

"You said you just wish…''

"Oh, oh, yes. Of course. I guess I just wish that Mitch wasn't different now.''

"Different?"

"He's so closed, so quiet. Maybe sad, I don't know."

Harley wouldn't have called him sad. Serious, maybe edgy, but sad? "Why's he sad?"

"That I don't know, dear. When he came here, Doc said he'd be helping out and installing a lab in the basement. God knows we can use one, but he stays in there a lot of the time, and when he's not in there, he's gone. But there's just something about him."

There was definitely "something" about him. Harley knew that after seeing him for just a short time. "What about his family?"

"Doesn't have any that I know of. His parents were gone when he came here."

"He—he's not married?"

"No, he's not—at least, I don't think so. He's never said, but I'm sure I'd know if he was." She smiled as she slipped the thermometer into a glass on the side table. "Now, I do remember he always had a way with the girls, though, with that voice and the way he has of looking—"

Harley interrupted her, not wanting to hear about Mitch's look or how women reacted to him. She had enough experience with both to know the woman was absolutely on the mark. "Mrs....?"

The nurse frowned. "Oh, I'm so sorry. I'm

Stella. And Doc told me you were having a bit of trouble with your memory.''

Harley could barely look at the woman now that the lie had spread. ''A bit of trouble.''

Stella patted her hand. ''Well, that'll pass. Just give it time. Now, is there anything I could get you? Some Jell-O, or a sandwich? There's a turkey in the oven, so you can have that later on, but how about something to tide you over?''

''Whatever you have would be fine,'' Harley said.

''Okay. You just lay back and take it easy, and I'll get you a snack.''

As the nurse hurried to the door, Harley called after her, ''Stella?''

She turned back. ''Yes, dear?''

''Where are the others?''

''Doc's on rounds, seeing the oldest Fisher boy. He cut his leg chopping wood, and Doc needed to go change the dressings. And Mitch...'' She glanced at her watch. ''He left a note that he was going to try and get to your car, to get your things out of it. He was gone when I got here, and it's almost three now and he's not back.'' She shrugged. ''Oh, well, he'll show up when he wants to. He usually does.'' Then she was gone.

Mitch had gone to the wreck to get her things, and Harley knew that the truth would be out very soon. Part of her was relieved to give up the charade, but a part of her didn't want anyone here knowing about her. When they found out, they wouldn't want her here anyway. So she'd get out of here now. It was a relief to settle that in her mind, and she was anxious to act on her plan.

She slipped out of the bed and looked around the room again to find her clothes. If she could get dressed, she'd be ready to go when Mitch got back. As she passed the windows, she hesitated, then went closer to look out at the land around the clinic. It was a white-on-white world, draped in snow and topped by a gray, wintery sky. The low buildings set away from the house were almost buried in the drifts, and the trees beyond were heavy limbed with snow and towered high into the heavens. Far off in the distance, she caught glimpses of mountains, their peaks shrouded by dark clouds.

She stared at the unbroken beauty, then was startled by a sudden flash of something, blurred movement in the trees—probably some deer or other animal. Then there was a color streak, something crashing out of the trees, shaking the snow from the lower branches. Then all movement stopped. And it wasn't a deer.

About ten feet from the dense undergrowth was a man standing in the virgin snow. Mitch. Even though he wore a heavy denim jacket and a watch cap pulled low over his long hair, she could tell it was him. He stood very still, his hands out in front of him, palms forward, fingers splayed, as if he was warding off something coming directly at him. But there was nothing there.

She watched as he slowly lowered his hands, pushed them into the pockets of his jacket. Then, as if he sensed her presence, he turned and looked directly at the window where she was standing. Even from that distance, she felt the impact of his gaze meeting hers. He held it for a long, tense moment, his head cocked to one side.

He'd been to her car, and he knew all about her. It was over, and a degree of relief washed through her. She wouldn't have to tell them why she was up here, or what she was going back to in Los Angeles. But she could thank them, pay them for everything they'd done for her, then leave. She waited for a greater relief at having this over and done with, but it didn't come.

As she looked out at Mitch, she had the strangest feeling she was leaving the only safe harbor she'd ever found in this world.

He saw her in the windows looking out at him. Her image shimmered in the frost-etched glass, making her look almost ethereal in the gown, with the darkness of her hair the only contrast in a white world. The sight of her almost took his breath away, adding to the tightness in his chest.

He couldn't remember where he'd been or what he'd done all day. Worse yet, he didn't know what she had seen from the window before he came to himself and realized she was there.

He turned to look behind him, but saw only his deep, blurred steps coming from the woods. And from the angle of the indentations in the snow, he knew he'd been running, and running hard. As he slowly turned back to the house, he saw that the window was empty. But she'd seen him.

Dammit all, he thought as he started toward the back entrance. He didn't need this, especially not after last night, when he'd bent the railing on the bed just because she'd touched his hand. He didn't need this at all. It was another episode of blacking out, and there were no links that he could find between the events. He had to figure it out, but first he had to find out what the woman had seen.

He reached the back porch, took the buried steps easily, then went inside, into a warmth that was almost suffocating. He stripped off his jacket quickly and hung it by the door, then skimmed off the cap and pushed it in a coat pocket. With one look at the door down to the lab, he passed it by and went directly to the woman's room.

WHEN HARLEY MOVED AWAY from the window, her foot struck a paper sack partially under the side table. She opened it and found her clothes neatly folded inside. She upended the bag on the bed, and was just about to take off the gown to get dressed when she heard someone in the hallway. The door opened, but it wasn't Stella with food.

Mitch strode into the room, his jacket and hat gone, and he was dressed in well-worn jeans, with a long-sleeved flannel shirt. High color touched his beard-roughened face, and his hair was skimmed back. He silently came toward her, and as he stopped at the foot of the bed, she was painfully aware she was dressed in nothing but a flimsy gown.

His narrowed eyes flicked over the clothes spilled out on the bed, then lifted to meet her gaze. She braced herself for that contact, waiting for the recognition, the reaction to her, but it wasn't there. There was something else in his hazel eyes, something she could only label as wariness. And she had no idea where it came from.

"What are you doing out of bed?" he asked.

This was the first time she'd faced him with them both standing, and although she was fairly tall for a woman, he was at least four inches taller than her five ten. It only added to her uneasiness. "I—I found my clothes and thought it was time to get dressed."

"I saw you at the window," he said abruptly.

She moved a bit closer to the bed and touched the lowered side rail with one hand. Her head felt a bit light, and she leaned against the railing for support. "I was just seeing what it was like out there."

"And what's it like?" he asked.

"Beautiful."

"Lots of snow, isn't there?"

"Lots," she murmured, then got closer to the bed and shifted to sit on the edge of it. She scooted back until her legs were dangling over the side, and she tugged at the short hem of the gown so it partly covered her thighs and hid all the bruises but the large one just above her knees. She wanted to get this over with. "Stella said you'd gone to get my things out of the car."

"Yes, I did."

She stared at her hands, smoothing the cotton on her legs, and asked, "You...you got them?"

"No."

She stared hard at her fingers as they stilled on the whiteness. "You left them there?"

"I couldn't get to them. The snow's buried everything for now."

She'd braced herself for the truth, to explain a bit to him, then try and make arrangements to leave. But that never came. He didn't know. He hadn't found her papers, or the portfolio she kept in the glove compartment, or the gun. And for a foolish moment, she let herself think of staying, maybe for a few more days, in a place where no one knew who she was and no one would ever know about her contact with Freeman.

But one look at Mitch and she knew it was time for her to go. The man was studying her with narrowed eyes, and the idea that she could get very used to seeing him and talking to him was unsettling. This wasn't her world—not even close—and she forced herself to do what she knew she should. "Can you tell me where to rent a car around here?"

He didn't answer her, and when she began to feel uneasy under his direct, silent scrutiny, she repeated, "There is a rental-car agency around here, isn't there?"

"Why?" he finally asked.

"I'll need some way to get out of here. Doc told me you thought my car was totaled, and now you said it's buried. So I won't be using it."

"No, it won't be going anywhere again."

"I'll need a rental car. Unless there's an airport close by?"

"There's no airport other than one that's just a pasture a local man uses for his single-engine plane. No jumbo jets, no terminals, no nothing."

"Then it's a car, I guess," she murmured.

"Lady, I don't understand you at all."

"Understand what?" she asked.

"Beyond the obvious—that you're not physically up to traveling yet, and this is a holiday and everything's shut down tight—there's the simple fact that you don't know who you are, so how do you know where you should be going? And even if you knew where to go, I assume that everything you have is in your car. So you don't have any money to rent a car or buy an airplane ticket."

She'd forgotten the simple logic of what he was saying and felt foolish, to say the least. "I wasn't thinking about all of that."

He stayed where he was by the foot of the bed, but that didn't lessen the effect of his intense scrutiny on her. "In a few days I'll be able to get to your car, and then we can talk about rental cars or buses, or getting in touch with a family member who can come and get you."

That was just what she'd thought about, and to hear him say it out loud took her aback. A few days. She could give herself a few days in this place. And she decided right then that she would. Then she'd walk away. She'd thought of going someplace to hide out and think, a place Freeman could never find her. And she'd stumbled on it the hard way.

So she didn't say anything else about leaving, and she didn't tell Mitch who she was. She just nodded. "You're right."

"Thanks for admitting that," he murmured, with the shadow of a smile playing around his lips.

"I'm the first to admit when I'm wrong," she said, wishing she could kid with him, and that the idea of him smiling at her wasn't so appealing right then. She slid off the bed, then grabbed at the side for support when her dizziness hit her.

As she held tightly to the rail, Mitch came to her side, but he didn't touch her. He hovered there, as if his presence was supporting her, then she took a deep breath and the world settled. That lasted until she looked at Mitch, inches from her, so close she could see a flare of gold in the iris of his eyes.

As if it had a life of its own, her hand reached out and touched him, her palm pressed to the softness of his flannel shirt over his heart. She could feel him almost flinch at the contact, but he didn't move away from her.

"Are you okay?" he asked, his voice a low rumble against her hand.

"Just—just a bit light-headed." She took a steadying breath, but nothing lessened the intensity of that contact or the feeling of his heart under her touch.

"Listen, I didn't save you from that wreck to have you keel over here because you don't know enough to stay in bed," he murmured.

She looked up at him. "You did save my life," she whispered. "I'm so thankful for that. I don't know how I can ever repay you."

He shook his head. "You don't owe me anything," he said.

His gaze pinned her to the spot, as if the touch of her hand on his chest anchored her, and that sense of safety was almost overwhelming. She'd never experienced anything like it before in her life. It was a unique, almost peaceful feeling, but over it all was the awareness of Mitch himself. A man who seemed to demand every iota of her attention. A man who filled the spaces around her just with his presence.

And she didn't want to let it go. Instead, she moved closer. She stood on her tiptoes and touched her lips to his. The contact shook her—that slight bristling of his beard against her face, the taste of him on her lips. The soft heat of his breath brushed against her, and any thought of the kiss being one of thanks was gone.

The contact ricocheted through her, every nerve in her alive and aware, and if Mitch had touched her, if his hands had found her, she knew she wouldn't have let go easily. But he didn't move. He stood very still under her touch, and as she realized that the kiss was all on her part, she felt heat burn her face and she moved back.

"Thank you," she whispered unsteadily, barely able to meet his gaze.

But when she did, she saw shock in the depths of his hazel eyes, and his jaw was clenched. She was mortified to have thrown herself at him like that, and looked away, moving back until her hips rested against the edge of the bed. She was embarrassed at how needy she'd been right then, and even more embarrassed when she realized that she'd wanted to kiss him ever since she'd woke and seen him in the shadows by the bed.

"I'm sorry, I..." she said, but her voice was unsteady and slightly breathless. "It's just I'm so grateful for everything...but I shouldn't have done that. I know that. It's just things are so crazy, so..."

Her voice trailed off as he just stared at her. More words wouldn't come, and she was infinitely thankful when he turned without a word and headed for the door. But it wasn't over that simply. When he got to the door, he turned and glanced back at her.

The overhead light shadowed his eyes and made them unreadable. As unreadable as his even-toned voice when he said, "I'll get your things for you as soon as I can, then you can ask Doc when you can leave."

"Leave? Who's talking about leaving?" someone asked right behind Mitch. Then Doc was there, looking around Mitch as he walked into the room carrying a small, covered tray. "What are you doing up, young lady? Stella told me you were out roaming around. Now I hear that you're thinking of leaving. Well, just forget it." He put the tray on the side table, then turned to Harley. "We have to make very sure you don't have any complications from the accident before you can even consider going anywhere. Now, sit down and let me take a good look at you."

She sank back on the bed and managed to utter, "I'm fine, really, I am."

Doc was right there, reaching for her wrist, and as he checked her pulse, she glanced at Mitch, still standing by the door. "You shouldn't be up like this," Doc was saying as he released her wrist. "Your heart's going a mile a minute and—" he touched her forehead with his hand "—you feel a bit overheated."

"I feel okay," she said, trying to block out the notion that if she touched her tongue to her lips, she'd taste Mitch there. "Really, I am."

"You're doing just fine, and I'm sure you could leave if someone was coming to get you. But leaving on your own is out of the question right now." Doc looked into her eyes, then reached for the thermometer and popped it in her mouth. "Actually, it's all closed down around here from the storm and the holiday. Besides, I've got a turkey in the oven. I can't promise it's going to be great, but it's going to be done soon."

He took the thermometer back, glanced down at it, then shook his head. "Normal. Odd, you feel a bit feverish." He put the thermometer back in the container by the bed, then touched her cheek. "Flushed."

"I told you, I'm fine."

He didn't look convinced, but motioned to the tray. "Stella made you up a snack to tide you over until dinner.'' He glanced at Mitch. ''Why don't you make sure she gets back in bed? I have to baste that turkey. That's what Stella told me before she took off. 'Baste the damned bird, Doc,' she said, 'and don't forget or it'll end up a dry old bird just like you.' That's the last thing we want.''

He crossed to Mitch, who hadn't moved, then looked back at Harley. ''Oh, I forgot, white or dark?''

''Excuse me?''

''Turkey meat—white or dark?''

''Oh, white, I guess. I think.''

''Great, that leaves the dark for me,'' he said with a smile, then looked at Mitch. ''We'll talk at dinner.''

''Later,'' Mitch murmured.

''You're going to be there for the meal, aren't you?''

''I've got work—''

''Not today you don't, son,'' Doc said. ''And no arguments. It's a holiday. A day of rest, or at least partial rest. Now, take care of her, and I'll call you both when dinner is ready.''

Doc left, and Harley looked at Mitch, as awkward as any teenager who had a crush revealed in the most embarrassing way. ''He's a very nice man,'' she said to fill the uncomfortable silence between them.

''He's more than nice,'' Mitch said. ''He's the

proverbial country doctor. He still makes house calls. He knows every patient, their kids and even their dogs.''

"One of a kind," she murmured.

"Damned right, he is." He stayed by the door, as if debating about coming back into the room. Then he moved abruptly to the bed. He swung the movable table toward Harley, then carefully picked up the covered tray and set it down in front of her.

"You need to eat," he said, but didn't offer to help her this time. She could feel the barrier raising again and she knew it was all her fault.

She ignored the tray in front of her and looked right at Mitch. "I meant it," she said. "I'm really sorry about what…what happened before Doc came in."

His hazel eyes narrowed on her, their intensity cutting through her. His hand moved toward her, as if to cup her chin, and as his gaze dropped to her parted lips, she thought this time he was going to kiss her.

Chapter Six

Mitch almost touched her. He almost let his fingers feel the sweep of her chin, the heat that seemed to radiate from her. And he almost bent over to taste her, to really taste her. She took a shuddering breath, and the action made her shoulders tremble. When her tongue touched her parted lips, he grabbed at sanity. He cut through the need in him that was fogging his reasoning and pulled back.

He closed his hand tightly in a fist, and with a very unsteady intake of air, turned from the sight of her, inches from him. His mind was reeling at what he'd almost done, and he moved farther from her, going to the windows, staring blindly out at the stark white landscape.

He pressed his clenched hands onto the sill of the window and closed his eyes to try and regroup. Control. God, he needed it right then, and he forced himself to stay there, to not turn when she finally spoke again. "It's crazy, isn't it?" she whispered.

Insane, he thought, but kept that to himself. "It's been an emotional time for you, a strange, stressful time for all of us." He was so close to the window that his breath fogged the glass as he spoke. "Things are out of whack and…things happen."

"I'm sorry."

He grimaced at her words. "Don't do that." He knew he should be the one apologizing, not her. He was the one who could have hurt her badly, the one who'd almost acted on a need rather than rational thinking.

"I guess I shouldn't say I'm sorry for saying I'm sorry, should I?"

He knew she was trying to make a joke, to break this horrible tension in the room, but he couldn't smile at all. "Something like that," he muttered. Then to prove to himself that he could have control, he lifted his hand and lightly touched the frosty glass with one finger.

The simple action made his hand shake, and he drew back. It wasn't the window he wanted to touch, and he knew that. And her being right there was seductive to him, so tempting. He had to get out of here and get out now. He drew his hand back, but before he could turn and escape, she stopped him with a soft statement. "No more apologies, just a thank-you for trying to get to my car this morning."

"I didn't get there," he said, more than aware

of the way the failing light was beginning to cast long shadows outside.

"You said it was buried by the snow?"

He'd forgotten he'd told her that. He'd gotten there—that he remembered—but he had no idea if he'd dug into the car or gone someplace else. So he improvised. "I meant I couldn't get into it, so I came back."

"Well, I appreciate it, and I mean that. It took you most of the day just to go there and back."

He wouldn't face the fact that the day was a blank to him. He raked both hands through his hair, then cupped them at the back of his neck and closed his eyes tightly for a moment. "It's a long way," he muttered.

He dropped his hands, then turned, but her words stopped him. She was on the bed still, the plate with the cover untouched, and she was hugging her arms around herself tightly. "Was something wrong out there?"

He narrowed his eyes, trying to minimize the effect just the sight of her had on him. "What?"

She shrugged, a fluttery, almost vulnerable action. "I saw you coming out of the woods, and it looked like there was a problem."

He cocked his head to one side, just watching her, waiting for a question from her that he wouldn't have an answer for. "Why?"

"You looked like something was chasing you."

He took a hissing breath. Why had he thought this was over and done? She'd seen him from the window, and now he was going to find out just what she actually had seen. It wasn't over and done any more than his gut reactions to her were a thing of the past. Far from it. "Why don't you tell me exactly what you saw?" he asked cautiously.

"I looked out, saw something in the woods, then you were there. You ran out, I think. I didn't really see you running, but you were there." She shook her head. "I don't know the woods around here, if there are deer or bears or something that could have been after you."

"There're deer, some bear."

"And you saw...?"

"No, I didn't. I was just anxious to get back." Then he took up one of her statements and made it his lie. "I'd been gone all day, and it was a long, hard trip."

"Sure," she murmured.

He could feel a sense of relief in him that she really hadn't seen anything incriminating. But that relief was quickly overlaid by something else when she pushed the tray away, swung her long legs over the side of the bed and sat there, facing him.

He nudged the tray out of his way, then went closer to her. "Is that it?" he asked. "Any more questions?"

She studied him with those deep blue eyes veiled

by incredibly long lashes. "Would you answer them?"

He shrugged. "What questions *haven't* I answered?"

"I've lost track."

He took another hissing breath, then realized that the best defense was a good offense. "Lady, I'll tell you anything you want to know about me when you tell me all about yourself."

The look in her blue eyes rocked him. Intense barely began to describe the look or his reaction when his gaze dropped to her lips again. He felt dizzy and off balance, and irrational. *Irrational and stupid,* he thought as his eyes flicked to hers again, and their expression was guarded.

"So, what if *I* tell you about myself?" she asked softly.

"Since you don't have a clue about yourself, that's hardly a viable offer."

Harley met his hazel gaze and knew she'd just been given her opening to tell him the truth about herself. The time to let whatever happened happen. To get it out in the open, then deal with whatever came. She slipped off the bed to stand and face him instead of having him looming over her in the bed. But when she moved, he jerked back as if afraid she'd touch him again.

For a minute they faced each other, mere inches separating them, and Harley felt her breath catch in her chest as his eyes flicked over her. The gown was uncomfortably skimpy right then, and she fought an urge to cross her hands over her breasts. The man had the most disconcerting way of just looking at her and making her feel as if he could see into her soul. As if she could taste his lips on hers. She had to force herself not to touch her lips with her tongue to see if his taste was still there.

She was barely aware of the gown slipping off her shoulder when she shrugged and said, "Mitch, I need to—"

He cut her off, snapping, "Get dressed," then turned abruptly and strode across the room. As he reached the door, he called over his shoulder, "Doc'll be back to let you know when dinner's ready." And he was gone.

And thankfully, she was saved from doing something foolish, like telling him the truth.

MITCH CLOSED THE DOOR to the lab, but that action didn't shut out the woman in the other room. For a moment the memory of her lips on his was there full force, and it made his body shudder. But no matter how much his body responded to her, his mind couldn't let go of the image of the bruises he'd seen again when her gown had slipped off her shoulder. Bruises he'd been responsible for inflicting on her.

Nothing could block that out. And that one image

gave him the grasp on sanity he needed. It gave him the ability to walk, to turn away from her and leave the room. But it didn't take away the need for her, which was so strong he couldn't understand it. He didn't know her name or anything else about her. He'd only known her for a day, but that need was very real.

He knew what lust was. He'd felt it often enough in his life, but this was different. It was a need. The need to touch her. He looked down at his hands and was unnerved to see that they were shaking. He pushed them into his pockets and did what he needed to do.

He crossed the lab, lined with metal shelves and stocked with the newest equipment, which he'd had shipped in. But when he tried to concentrate, to enter the happenings of today in the computer, he found his mind drifting. Finally, he sat back at the desk by the high windows blocked by snow, and stared at the empty blue screen.

He shook his head, then quickly typed in what had happened today—the clinical version of his blackout and the ensuing problems. And he never mentioned the woman. He finished with the cursor blinking after the words *memory loss, or total blackouts?* He didn't know. He didn't have any answers. All he knew for sure was that the effects of the formula weren't wearing off, but were intensifying, along with side effects he hadn't anticipated.

Blackouts, and inability to control his pressure on objects. He could do it if he concentrated. Touching things, feeling things, using dishes and even the computer. But if he once lost concentration, he knew the damage he could do would be beyond repair. He'd managed to feed her soup last night by focusing. But then she'd touched his hand and that concentration had flown. And the rail had been bent. The memory of bruises on a pale shoulder made him shiver.

He determinedly blocked that out and reached for a water glass he'd left on the desk. He held it in one hand, the pressure easy and sure. He kept the pressure at a steady tension as he stared long and hard at his fingers closed around the glass. They looked so normal it could almost fool him into thinking he wasn't dangerous to other people.

A knock sounded on the lab's outer door, and Mitch stood with the glass in his hand and went to answer it. Doc was there, dressed as if he'd been outside, in his heavy jacket and fur hat. "I was beginning to think you'd fallen asleep," he said with a touch of reproach.

"What's going on?"

"I got a call from the Fosters. Ellen, their oldest girl, burned herself cooking the big dinner, and I need to run out there to see how bad it is."

"Can't they bring her in?"

Doc shook his head. "Oh, my boy, they've got

six kids. Do you know how much that would ruin things for them if Butch had to leave to bring her here? It's not that far and much easier for me to just pop over and check it out."

"Have you looked out the window lately?"

"You're buried down here, but the snow's let up. It's not that bad out, and the old truck can get through. I just came to let you know where I'll be if there's any problems and to tell you the food's all ready. You and our guest go ahead and eat, and I'll get back when I can."

"We can wait."

"No, you can't. It's all on the stove and in the warming oven. If you wait for me, the whole meal will be dried out. Eat, enjoy, and take care of things while I'm gone," he said with a smile. Then the smile turned to a frown. "Hey, I'm asking you to have a great meal with a beautiful woman. You look as if I've asked you to jump off a tall building and land on a six-inch sponge. What's going on?"

Mitch avoided a direct answer. "Food. We'll have food," he said.

"Good. I'll be back as soon as I can, and if there's a problem, I'll call," he said, then went back down the hallway.

Mitch hesitated by the door, debating about ignoring Doc's instructions and just shutting himself inside the lab again. But he finally closed and locked the door, then went upstairs to the woman's room.

He got to the door and knocked carefully on the wood with his knuckles. But there was no answer. He knocked again, then, afraid that something had happened to her, he opened the door and stepped inside.

He glanced at the bed, and at the same moment he realized she wasn't there, but her clothes were laid out on the rumpled linen, he heard the bathroom door open. He turned and saw her coming out of the steamy room, her hair loose and wild around her slightly flushed face. She was wearing only a skimpy lace bra and panties.

She registered his presence at the same time he realized that any impact she'd had on him up to that moment was insignificant compared to the suddenly intense reaction he had at the sight of her now. When she turned those huge blue eyes on him, he could feel his mouth go dry and his whole body stir.

He started to apologize and back out, but any words were cut off by her gasp. "Oh, my God," she cried, staring at his hand.

He looked down. The glass he'd been holding was crushed. Blood was everywhere, and when he slowly opened his fingers, the shards fell to the floor with the pooling blood. He saw a jagged cut across his palm, from the base of his thumb to his ring finger. And he'd never felt it happen. Any ideas he'd entertained that he could control himself were shattered with the glass.

Harley was frozen at the sight of the blood and the jagged wound on Mitch's hand. For a moment she couldn't move, then she hurried toward him, not knowing what to do, but knowing she had to do something.

"Oh, Mitch," she breathed, and reached out. But before she could touch his bloody hand, he jerked it back and spun away from her to go to the closet on the far wall.

"I'll go and get Doc," she said, more than aware of the blood and glass on the floor by the open door.

"He's gone," Mitch grunted as he jerked open the closet with his good hand, then fumbled inside.

She hurried after him, and when she got close to him, she could see he was grabbing a bunch of large gauze pads stacked on the top shelf. "Where's Doc?" she asked. "I'll go and get him."

"Gone, on an emergency." He flexed his gashed hand, then pushed the thick pile of cotton against his injury as he motioned with his head to the closet. "Get some tape out of there for me. Bottom shelf on the right. Wide tape."

She did as he told her, then turned and was taken aback to see Mitch with his eyes tightly closed and his jaw clenched. His good hand gripped the other, and the blood was already soaking through the cotton and staining his fingers.

Quickly, she pulled off a long piece of tape and reached for his hand. As she touched him, his eyes opened abruptly, and she was the one to jerk back at the contact. His skin was icy cold, and for a moment it stunned her.

"You're so cold. You—you could be going into shock," she said.

He shook his head. "It's not shock." He eased the blood-soaked cotton off the wound, and she saw the cut, jagged and gaping. Then he dropped the bloody pads and reached for more. He pressed them to his palm, then held out his hand to her. "Just put it on good and tight."

She felt awkward, trying to loop the thick tape around his hand, and she didn't miss the way the cotton rapidly stained with the blood. "You're bleeding so much, I don't—" He shivered suddenly and she stopped, looking up at him. "Mitch?"

He shook his head as if to clear it. "It's okay, just get it over with."

She went back to wrapping the tape around and around his palm. "Are you sure this is—"

"Yes, I'm sure. Just do it tighter."

"You're shaking and I don't want to hurt you."

His tongue touched his lips and he breathed, "You couldn't hurt me if you tried. Now, just do it."

She concentrated on the taping, pulling it as tightly as she could, then finished by crossing the tape on the back of his hand. Then she supported his hand and gazed at her pitiful job of bandaging. "Boy, it looks awful. I wish I knew something about first aid."

When the shivering hit him, Mitch had had the strangest feeling that he was losing something. But he had no idea what. Then he felt her touch, and whatever had almost happened was stopped before it had begun. Shock. Maybe she'd been right, but he'd never experienced anything like it. Then his mind cleared, and he could feel the cutting pain in his hand, her holding him and the tightness of the bandage around the wound.

"You did just fine," he managed to say as he drew back from her support.

"Are you sure that's going to be enough? You might need stitches or get an infection or something."

He looked at the makeshift bandage. "Don't worry about it."

"Well, if you're sure?"

He cradled his sore hand in his other one and pulled it against his shirt, which was more than a little stained with the blood. "I'm the doctor around here. Let me worry about details. You did just fine."

"Do you need anything else?"

He looked back at her, and the answer that came rocked him. He needed her. He backed away from the impact of that thought, but couldn't hide from the sight of her in front of him. He couldn't forget what had happened when he'd first entered this room and seen her. Self-protectively, he narrowed his eyes in an attempt to lessen any impact on him caused by the sight of her now in the indecently skimpy clothes.

But it didn't help. There was still the sweep of her throat, her naked shoulders, her small high breasts barely contained by the lacy bra. And the reaction in his body was definitely not diminished. He was actually thankful for the pain in his hand for giving him something to concentrate on. Then another pain overlapped it as he glanced down at the bruises that still marred the delicate skin of her upper arm. "I'll be fine," he murmured. He focused on the tape and the stained cotton. "Just fine."

"If you're sure…?"

He made himself look at her and stay very still. "Lady, it's okay. I'm fine. I'll go and clean up, and you…you can get dressed."

He could literally see color touch her cheeks as he spoke, and he wondered when was the last time he'd seen a woman blush. "Oh, yes, sure. I—I…"

She turned to head for the bed and her clothes, but in that instant he saw her bare feet—and the glass and blood in her path. He moved without thinking, lunging to one side, putting out his arm to block her from stepping into the jagged shards of glass. "Watch out!"

In the next instant he felt her run into his forearm, her softness hitting him, then he saw her stagger backward and, thankfully, catch the edge of the closet door with one hand. She steadied herself, her blue eyes wide, and stammered, "What—why did you do that?"

"The glass. I thought..." He shook his head, feeling the sting from the impact in his arm and knowing that she had to have felt it, too. Even when he was trying to help, he hurt her.

She pressed a hand to her chest as she righted herself, then looked at the floor. "Oh, God, I didn't even think." She turned the blueness of her eyes on him. "You're making a habit out of this, aren't you?"

"Out of what?"

"Saving me from things."

He was making a habit out of hurting her, and that thought nauseated him. She was made to be loved and cherished, not bruised and knocked over. "I broke the damn thing in the first place."

"How did it happen?" She rubbed absentmindedly at her breastbone just above the lacy fringe of her bra. "I saw you, then the blood."

"It didn't just break, it shattered," she said.

He barely covered a shiver and found himself backing up a bit, needing to get some distance. "It's broken, that's for sure." He wanted out of here, now. "Thanks for helping."

"It's the least I could do, after everything you've done for me."

Done to you, he thought with a bitter taste rising in his throat. "Consider us even now."

"Putting on a bandage hardly qualifies as saving your life."

"Let me be the judge of that."

"Mitch, if you hadn't found me, I wouldn't be around to do anything for you."

"Lady, don't you ever give up and let me have the last word?"

She shrugged, a fluttery movement of her naked shoulders. "I guess I'm a bit stubborn."

"That's an understatement."

The smile came suddenly, and its impact on him seemed to get stronger and stronger each time he saw it. Odd that he didn't even know her name, and she could shake his world with an expression. He didn't know where she came from, or if some man woke to this smile every morning and went to sleep with it every night. A man who wouldn't hurt her, a man who could touch her.

Mitch turned away as his breathing tightened,

and carefully walked over to the door. "I'll be back to clean up this mess as soon as I change."

"I'll do it," she said from across the room.

Mitch got to the door, avoiding the glass and blood on the floor, and as he took a step out into the hall, he felt as if the temperature dropped twenty degrees. He shivered violently, closing his eyes to try and absorb it, then reached blindly for the door jamb for support.

He tried to breathe, tried to get air into his lungs, and it began to ease whatever was happening to him. The chill started to lift, and whatever had gripped him gradually dissolved into nothingness, as if it had never been. Slowly, he let go of the door jamb, drawing his good hand back to cradle the injured one. Then he turned, afraid she'd be there with her questions and her touch.

But she was nowhere in sight. Her clothes were gone from the bed, and the bathroom door was shut. He could hear water running in the other room, and he breathed a sigh of relief that she hadn't witnessed what had just happened to him. He couldn't explain it to himself, much less to her. And if she had seen it, she wouldn't have ignored it. Not with her overdeveloped sense of owing him, of needing to make things up to him.

Then the door opened and she was there, dressed in slim jeans, her shirt buttoned but untucked. In bare feet, with her hair curling damply around her face, she stopped when she saw him standing in the hallway. She was holding a rag and a bottle of cleaner she must have found in the bathroom. "Oh, I didn't realize you were..." Her voice trailed off as she glanced at his still-bloody clothes. "I thought you were going to change?"

To him it had only been a moment, but she'd managed to shower and dress and find the cleaning supplies. "I am...I was," he murmured. He was confused. Then he realized that it had happened again, right in the hallway. Time gone, lost to him. And it could have happened in front of her.

He didn't have a clue how long he'd been there in the doorway. But one glance at the wood, and he could see indentations in the frame from his grip on it. He tried to act as if nothing had happened and to speak as if nothing was wrong, even though he could taste fear in his throat.

Chapter Seven

Harley was looking at him expectantly, and Mitch grasped at words. "I—I forgot to tell you why I came in here in the first place."

She came closer, but stayed on the other side of the mess on the floor. "Oh, why?"

"Dinner. Doc said it's ready."

"He's here? I thought you said—"

"No, he's not here. The kid of one of his patients burned herself, and he went to help. But before he left, he gave orders for us to have dinner and not wait for him to get back. If you aren't hungry, you could—"

"I am. I'm very hungry, actually."

"The food's in the kitchen. Doc said it's all ready."

"I'll just be a few minutes cleaning up," she said.

He nodded, then turned and walked away down the hallway. He tried not to think, to just go into his room, strip off his bloody clothes and wash up as well as he could with the awkward bandage wrapped around his hand.

By the time he'd dressed in a plain white T-shirt and fresh jeans, he felt as if he'd regained some control. His hand felt fine, and whatever had happened was over. No more chills, no more black moments. At least he prayed it was over as he made his way to the kitchen.

Mitch stepped into the room redolent with the smell of fresh roast turkey, and memories from the past flooded over him. Of the cavernous room with its huge table set for Thanksgiving with twenty plates and cups, and Doc at the head, carving two fat turkeys. Of the fresh flowers Mrs. Barnette always found for the occasion. Of kids clamoring for the drumsticks, piling their plates with mashed potatoes and yams, then the pumpkin pies.

Now the room was just as big, and the table just as large, sitting by the bay windows at the back. But there were just three place settings at the far end, though Doc had bought some daisies, put them in a glass jar and set them by the plates.

The same room, the same holiday, but what a change. Mitch crossed to the stove and methodically concentrated on putting food on the table with his good hand. Just as he set out the sliced turkey, he sensed that she was there, the same way he'd sensed her watching him from the window earlier. He turned, thinking he was prepared for her arrival.

He was prepared in one way. He could look at her and realize how lovely she was standing there just inside the door. What he wasn't prepared for was an aching loneliness that came with that sight, something he'd never experienced before, not even when he'd been here at the orphanage those long years ago. She'd brought that loneliness with her from wherever she'd come from in her red Jeep, brought it to him with her blue eyes and midnight hair and soft lips.

He motioned to the table. "Doc left a feast," he said. "And it's ready."

She came into the room, and as he sat at the side of the table with his back to the window, she took the chair facing him. She glanced at the food, then up at him. "It looks wonderful."

He nudged the plate of turkey toward her. "Help yourself."

She chose some turkey, then a little bit of the food in each serving dish on the table. As she ate, her lips seemed to hold a half smile. All he could think of was the touch of those lips on his. For God's sake, he couldn't even touch a plate without worrying about grinding it to dust, or touch a door frame without leaving evidence of his strength, and he was letting his mind wander into places he knew he shouldn't go.

"Mmm," she said softly as she tasted one of the rolls. "This is wonderful."

"If you want wine, there's some in the refrigerator."

She went to get it and he was struck by how she moved. Quietly, almost elegantly, even in rumpled jeans, a mussed shirt and with bare feet. She turned to look at him, her long lashes partially shadowing her blue eyes. "White? Is that okay with you?"

He could have used a bit of the fuzziness that came from alcohol right then, but knew he couldn't take the chance of losing what little control he still had. "Whatever you like," he said. "I don't want any. I'm not much of a wine drinker."

She came back to the table and poured the pale liquid into her goblet. "All I know about wine is white with chicken, red with beef."

"What about turkey?"

She held up her partially full goblet and looked at him over the rim. "Poultry. White." She lifted the glass in his direction. "Cheers."

"Cheers," he echoed with a nod.

"What a shame Doc has to be gone," she said as she put her goblet back down on the table.

"Drawback of the profession." Mitch picked up a serving spoon with his left hand and awkwardly managed to get some mashed potatoes on his plate. Before he could finish, she'd come around to him.

"You fed me," she said. "The least I can do is

dish your food up for you." Before he could object, she had the turkey platter and was putting some of the meat on his plate. "Dark meat," she said, then reached for the peas and carrots. "How about vegetables?"

"Sure," he said, thankful that he didn't have to manipulate the utensils.

Without asking, she picked up his knife and cut the turkey into smaller pieces, then buttered his bread and pushed the plate closer to him. "There you go. All set."

Mitch looked from the food to her as she went back to sit in the other chair again. As she settled, he spoke without thinking. "No airplane game?"

That brought a smile from her that had the same effect as the sun coming out on a dreary day. "Do you want me to play it with you?"

"I think I'll manage without it," he said, gripping the fork carefully and spearing a piece of the meat.

"There, you're doing just fine," she said. "But eat slowly, and if you need me to cut up more for you, just ask."

He let the fork rest on his plate and sat back. "I'm a big boy."

"How old are you?"

"Thirty-five."

She nodded. "Yes, I guess you qualify as a big boy." The accompanying smile was there, and he didn't feel particularly mature at that moment. He felt more like some stupid teenager with raging hormones.

"How old are you?"

"Twenty-eight on Christmas Day," she said easily, then her hand stilled as it broke off another piece of the roll, and her blue eyes flashed to his face. "I—I mean, I think..." She pushed aside the roll and nibbled on her bottom lip. "That's odd. I mean, it just came to me."

High color touched her cheeks, and he had the most disconcerting feeling that she was fearful. But there was no reason to be afraid. "You're remembering," he said. "That's good."

"Yes, I guess so," she murmured, and picked up the wine goblet to take a drink. He didn't miss the way her hand shook slightly or the way she covered it with her other hand.

"What's wrong?" he asked, watching her closely.

She put the glass down, then sat back. "I'm just...it's so odd for me. All of this."

When her eyes met his, he knew it was more than things being odd. Then he knew something that he had no way of knowing. It just came to him, and he knew it was a fact. "You remember, don't you?"

"Excuse me?"

"You remember who you are, where you came from, don't you?"

She looked away, at her hands pressed to the tabletop, and was silent for a long moment. Then she glanced up at him. He didn't know what he expected, but it wasn't her saying in a low voice, "Yes, I do."

He'd sensed it, but her admission shocked him. "Everything?"

"Everything."

"God, why didn't you say something before this?"

She hesitated, and he had that same sense of fear in her. "I almost...I was going to. I just wasn't really sure if I should."

"Who are you?"

Harley had thought of telling him before, but now that it came right down to it, she held back. There was so much to lose and so much trouble that could come out of this admission. She didn't want any of that trouble visiting this place. And after the kiss, his accident... So much had happened. But she knew she couldn't back down now.

"I'm Harley Madison."

She said the words and waited for him to recognize the name. But all he did was repeat in that low, rough voice, "Harley? As in the motorcycle?"

Nothing. No recognition. And she'd been so worried, so concerned. "Actually, my real name's Han-

nah, but I haven't been called Hannah for years."
She tried to laugh, but the sound was tight and nervous in her own ears. "My father was a big fan of motorcycles, and I was the sixth kid, and he always said that he didn't think the name Hannah was quite right for someone who was born after he drove my mom to the hospital on his Harley. So I sort of got this nickname that stuck."

He studied her long and hard, and she knew that all of her fears about saying her name earlier had been foolish. Even with her name, he didn't know who she was. "Well, you certainly don't look like a Harley," he finally murmured.

"What *do* I look like?"

He shrugged, his shoulders testing the cotton of his T-shirt. "I don't know," he said, then asked, "are you married?"

"No, I'm not."

He looked away from her, down at his plate, and picked up his fork with the piece of turkey still on it. "A day for revelations," he murmured as he awkwardly held his fork.

Revelations that didn't seem to amount to much of anything, she thought with real relief. Then she asked, "Do you need help?"

He cast her a shadowed look from under his dark brows, those hazel eyes narrowed on her. "Excuse me?"

"With your food. You fed me, so I could feed you."

He let his fork drop on his plate with a clatter and sat back in his chair, his head cocking to one side and that squint narrowing his eyes. "Lady, do you always do that?"

"Do what?"

"Keep score. I did this for you, so you do that for me? If I do something, you have to do something to pay me back."

"I didn't mean..." She shrugged, the idea of owing him on any level not something she was comfortable with at all. "I guess you're right."

"You've got some deep-seated need to make sure you never owe anyone anything, don't you?"

She was shocked that he'd almost read her mind. Was it so obvious? "You never said what sort of doctor you actually are. A psychiatrist?"

"No, not even close."

"A chiropractor?"

That brought the suggestion of a smile, and it lifted Harley's mood as Mitch said, "No, afraid not. If you have a sore neck, I can't do a thing for you."

"You never said if you want me to feed you."

He studied her for a long moment, then sat forward and reached for his turkey with his fingers. "No, thanks. I can manage."

"No, don't eat that yet. I forgot. This is Thanksgiving, and you're supposed to say what you're thankful for in your life before you eat.''

He paused with the piece of turkey in his hand. ''Another game like airplane?''

''No, I'm serious. You know, what you're grateful for. We used to do it at the table on Thanksgiving.''

''You get back your memory and one thing you remember is some holiday ritual?''

''It's tradition, not ritual. There's a difference.''

''Okay, I'll give you that. Now where did it come from?''

''Texas.''

''That's where you came from?''

''Originally.''

''Lady, you're a long way from Texas. How did you get out here?''

''I haven't lived in Texas for years, since I was eighteen.''

''Why did you leave?''

''I went out to Los Angeles to make my fortune,'' she said honestly.

One dark eye brow lifted in her direction. ''And did you make your fortune?''

''I'm doing okay.''

''So, what do you do that's making you a fortune?''

''I didn't say I *had* a fortune, I said I'm doing okay.''

"At what?"

She didn't want to lie anymore to him, but found herself hedging the truth just a bit. "I work in photography."

"Ah, so that's how a person makes a fortune these days?"

"That's how I make my living."

"Okay. You're making your fortune at photography." He held up the piece of turkey. "Can I eat now?"

"No, you haven't said what you're thankful for."

Mitch never took his eyes off Harley as the answer to that question came with no trouble at all. He was thankful he'd found her, and that she was safe and that she was here. And he wouldn't think about tomorrow, when she'd be gone. "Do I have to?"

"If you want to eat," she said with a teasing gleam in her eyes.

"Okay." So he told her a truth, but not the one that had just come to him. "I'm thankful for Doc and this place."

"This is all pretty important to you, isn't it?"

"It's the only home I had, such as it was back then, and Doc was the closest thing I ever had to a father. Yes, I'm thankful for him," he said, and meant it. He nodded to Harley. "Now it's your turn. What is Harley Madison thankful for?"

Without missing a beat, she said, "You."

He almost dropped the turkey, but recovered enough to lay it on his plate before he said, "Excuse me?"

"You. Mitch." She frowned. "You know, I don't think you ever told me your last name."

"Rollins."

"Okay, Mitch Rollins. I'm thankful for you for finding me and bringing me here."

He felt more than uneasy about her words and the look of intensity on her face. "I just did what anyone would do."

"Like a plumber?"

It took him aback to hear her say what Doc had said that night. "What?"

"I have this vague memory of someone calling you a plumber or maybe you calling yourself a plumber." She looked puzzled. "I don't know if it happened or not, just like the things after the crash."

"What things?" he asked, his food all but forgotten.

"You won't laugh if I tell you, will you?"

"No, what things?"

"When I was in the car, I had these weird hallucinations. Crazy things, like someone lifting the car and rolling it over. And the door being torn off. Then I was flying."

He could feel his stomach tightening more with

each word she uttered. "Anything else? Like what happened for you to go off the road?"

"No, just something ran in front of me. I braked and everything went out of control."

He'd been down that way that night, going so far he'd run back in the dark. He'd crossed the road, but he hadn't seen anything. "What ran out in front of you?"

"I don't know. I think I saw something, but it's all blurred, in motion. I can't remember that part of it. I just remember sliding and falling." She shivered. "Then I was trapped for what seemed forever before I felt the car rolling and..." She grimaced a bit. "You know, all that crazy stuff I imagined."

Mitch couldn't even factor the possibility that he might have crossed the road and caused her to skid, and was gone so quickly he hadn't heard anything happening behind him. No, he couldn't face that at all. "Well, you have some pretty wild hallucinations, I'll give you that. Especially the flying one."

"It was more like soaring or something. Sort of like Superman."

He looked down at his food and knew he couldn't eat any of it now. "Superman? And were you Lois Lane?"

She laughed softly at that, a sound that only made his tension increase. "I wasn't anyone, just there, being carried. It was all crazy and mixed up, then I was safely here."

Safe? No matter what he'd done or not done, he'd at least been able to get her back here without too much damage. "Lady, I can tell you I brought you back here, and we definitely didn't fly."

She cast him a veiled look from under her long lashes. "I told you it was crazy." She fingered the fork by her plate. "But tell me something."

"What's that?"

"How did you get me out of the car? I don't remember much, but I do know the car was top down and crushed. I remember trying to reach the door, but I couldn't quite touch it. Then I knew I couldn't open it even if I was free. It was all mashed down and into the frame. I was just wondering how you managed to get me out of there."

"You remember everything now, don't you?"

"Enough about hanging upside down."

He tried to keep eye contact while he lied to her. "It wasn't as bad as you remember. The door almost fell off, and I managed to get you out, then bring you back."

She sat back with a soft sigh. "Whatever you did, I am very thankful for it."

He fingered the bandage on his right hand. "And I'm thankful for you helping me with this."

She smiled suddenly, and he was amazed at how just an expression from her could alter and shift everything. "Now who's talking paybacks?"

"Okay, okay, let's leave it at that," he said, and

quickly looked away from her to his food. He picked up the turkey again. "Now that's over, let's eat," he said, then popped it into his mouth.

"I'm starving."

"That sounds like a very good sign," someone said from across the room, and Mitch looked up to see Doc coming into the room in his heavy outer clothes. "And you look wonderful." The elderly man smiled at Harley.

"You finally made it back," Mitch said.

"Just for a short time. I needed to get more supplies, and I think I'll be staying the night at the Fishers just to keep an eye on the girl. She's a bit shocky, and the parents are so upset. The mother blames herself, and the younger kids are scared to death. Not a great holiday for any of them."

"You have to eat with us," Harley said. "After all, you made all this food."

"Oh, Stella helped me out. I'll have leftovers tomorrow, and meanwhile, Mrs. Fisher is keeping me very well fed at her place. So you're doing much better, obviously."

"She's doing better than that," Mitch said. "She remembers everything. Doc, meet Harley Madison."

"Oh, it's my pleasure," he said. "It all came back to you, did it?"

"Yes," she murmured.

"Harley—what a unique name."

"After the motorcycle," Mitch said.

The doctor laughed. "What a beautiful woman to be named after a motorcycle. Well, Harley, enjoy the meal. I'll just go and get my things from the supply room to refill my bag, then be on my way."

"Before you leave, could you take a look at Mitch's hand?"

Mitch hadn't realized that he'd put his injured hand out of sight under the table until Harley mentioned it. "That's not necessary at all."

Doc looked at him as Harley said, "He cut it on a broken glass, and there's a really bad gash across his palm."

Mitch laid his hand on the table by his plate, palm down. "It's nothing. We bandaged it up and the bleeding's stopped."

Doc moved closer and frowned at the bandaged hand. "Mitch, why didn't you say something?"

"You're in a hurry, and I don't need—"

"I've got time for this," he said, and pulled out the next chair. He put his bag on the floor, then looked at Mitch. "Okay, son, let's take a look at the damage you did."

Mitch held his hand out, resting it on the table, and glanced at Harley as she got up and came around to lean over Doc's shoulder. Doc took scissors out of his bag, then methodically snipped the tape off and gently eased away the bloodstained cotton.

Mitch looked up at Harley, who was intent on what Doc was doing. Her tongue was caught between her teeth, and she grimaced when Doc peeled the last piece of cotton away from the wound. Then her eyes widened and she whispered, "Oh, my God, what...?"

Mitch glanced down at his hand and felt an echo of Harley's surprise. The jagged gash that he knew needed stitches was gone, and in its place was a narrow cut that was almost closed and looked as if it barely separated the skin at all. No gaping wound. No torn tissue. No swelling. No infection. Nothing. Just an almost-healed hand.

Harley shook her head, leaning even closer to get a better look. "It was all jagged and horrible and bleeding all over the place," she breathed. "I don't understand. It can't be. This is crazy."

"Well, it doesn't look too bad," Doc said as he reached back in his bag and took out disinfectant and a simple Band-Aid. "Not bad at all. How did you say you did it?"

"He did it on a broken glass," Harley said. "But this isn't the cut. I mean, he crushed this glass in his hand and there was blood all over and the wound was horrible. Just awful."

"Then he's damned lucky it didn't cut a lot worse than this," Doc said as he dabbed at the wound with a cotton swab dipped in a tiny brown bottle.

Harley felt as if she was caught in some parallel universe, a mirror image that was distorted. The cut wasn't the one she'd helped bandage. She looked at Mitch, needing some confirmation that she hadn't imagined the whole thing. But he was staring at his hand, as if he couldn't believe it, either.

"Mitch, what's going on?"

When he looked up and she met his hazel gaze, her world crumbled. "It just looked a lot worse than it was," he said. "It's nothing."

Chapter Eight

"Oh, no!" Harley backed up. "That's crazy. I saw it. It was bleeding and terrible and cut so deeply. Blood was all over the floor."

"Glass wounds bleed a lot sometimes," Doc said as he picked up the Band-Aid, then dropped it back in his bag. "You don't need it. It looks just fine."

"No, listen to me," she said, feeling as if she was falling into some black hole where there was nothing to hold on to. "I'm telling you, that wound was deep and terrible and ugly, and I was so worried. It bled and bled, and Mitch, he had to use all sorts of pads...."

Her words died out when she realized that both men were looking at her as if she'd lost her mind. As if she was imagining things. "I know what I saw," she said, but there was less conviction in her voice now. She'd thought she'd seen Superman, too. That she'd flown. But the cut... She took a shuddering breath. "I was sure..."

"It *is* fine," Mitch said as he stood. "It bled a lot, but it wasn't serious. I told you that," he said, his hazel eyes narrowed on her. "Just don't let it upset you like this. It's no big thing."

"No big thing," she whispered.

"You didn't have to bother with it, Doc." He glanced at his friend, then back to Harley, his expression guarded. The man she'd been talking to over dinner was gone as if he'd never been here with her. The barriers were once again firmly in place. "I really need to make a call." With that, he crossed the kitchen and left.

As Doc stood and turned, Harley met his gaze. She hated the concern in his eyes. Concern for her sanity, no doubt. "Doc, I was so sure." She still was, but there was no way she could say any more to him. "I'm sorry."

His voice held a patronizing tone when he said, "Harley, to the layperson, wounds can look terrible when they really aren't. You saw blood and over-reacted, that's all."

"But I..." She bit her lip. "He was so cold. I remembered something about shock and I thought he...that Mitch was in shock or something."

"Not from a little wound like that. And his body temperature felt just fine to me." He shrugged. "You know, after what you've been through, I'm not surprised that things are...a little mixed up for you. When you have hypothermia, sometimes you can get a chemical imbalance. It's hard to readjust. So this could be that or a touch of delayed reaction to your own situation."

It sounded so logical when he put it like that, and she felt so illogical right then. The way she had since the accident. "I guess you're right."

"I'm no psychiatrist, but I'd say you should finish your dinner, then get to bed and take it easy. I'll be back in the morning to check on you. Oh, did you get through to your relatives, to let them know you're all right?"

"No, there isn't anyone I need to call," she admitted.

He frowned slightly. "Are you sure?"

"Yes, I was just driving to get away for a while. I don't have to be anywhere until Monday."

"Then where do you have to be?"

"Los Angeles."

"Well, that won't be a problem. Tomorrow we can see about getting you back there. Now don't look so worried. We'll take care of it just fine for you. We'll get you back to your family and your normal life. But for now just rest and get better."

She tried to erase a frown she knew was tugging at her face, but it didn't come from worry about getting back to Los Angeles. It was the cut on Mitch's hand, and the way she was beginning to wonder what she'd really seen. Hallucinations. God, she just wished that they would stop.

"Thank you," she breathed. But she couldn't quite forget the blood dripping from his hand and that jagged wound.

"Now, you sit down and finish eating. I'll be back first thing in the morning. Tell Mitch for me that there aren't any appointments tomorrow, so I gave Stella the day off. He just needs to monitor calls until I get back. Okay?"

"Yes, of course." As he turned to leave, Harley said, "Doc, when I get my things from the car, I'll pay you for all of this."

"Don't worry about that now. We'll work something out," he said, then he was gone.

Harley took one look at her barely touched food, then sat down by it. "Forget it," she told herself. "Just forget it. Forget it and Superman and flying." She managed to eat a bit more before she pushed the plate away.

Mitch hadn't come back by the time she'd put everything in the fridge and headed to her room.

She felt vaguely disoriented. Maybe she really had hallucinated the wound. Maybe she had hallucinated Mitch running out of the woods so quickly she hadn't realized he was there until he was standing so still in the snow by the old barns. She knew for sure that she'd been hallucinating when she thought Superman had rescued her. She almost laughed at that. Superman. Sure, and she was going back to a family and her normal life.

But she wouldn't have much of a life at all if she didn't placate Freeman. And that meant giving him what she had for the rest of her life. Her stomach hurt, and she wished she hadn't tried to eat any more. As she went into her room, she swung the door shut behind her, then stopped and stared at the floor.

It was faint, but she could still make out a stain. She crouched down and touched it with the tip of her finger. It was real, all right. She didn't have any idea whether everything else she thought she'd seen was real or not. But Mitch had the answers.

MITCH WORKED IN THE LAB for hours, checking his blood, his vitals, studying the closure on the wound, scanning it, and trying to figure out what he'd stumbled onto. Before, he'd thought he'd created a monster, a way to make superarmies, where soldiers could go for days at top speed and win battles just by sheer endurance. Now there was something else.

If the healing was caused by the serum, all sorts of new possibilities would be opened. Armies that couldn't be stopped by minor wounds. Armies that could be invincible. A real nightmare in the wrong hands, but a miracle for all humanity in the right ones.

He worked through the evening, and when he finally knew what his next step had to be, it was almost nine o'clock and he was more than ready to go ahead. He prepared a sterile environment at his main work station, set up the video camera he'd been using to keep a living log of his progress, then laid out everything he needed.

Stripped down to just his jeans, he turned on the camera, then sat on the bench at the table and started talking, giving a list of all the instruments he had next to him and the testing he'd do when he had started the process.

Resting his right arm on the table, he said, "Tape 22, 9:06, Thanksgiving evening." He opened his hand and looked at it. The cut was healed almost completely now, leaving just a thin pink line across the palm. "Of all the possibilities I thought of when I started working on my original theory, none involved spontaneous healing. Endurance for survival was the core target. But now it appears that spontaneous healing is a distinct side effect that could be an even more compelling reason to proceed with the research."

He picked up a scalpel with his left hand, steadied it, then said, "To see if that's a valid possibility, I am going to do a control test...."

HARLEY STAYED IN HER ROOM as long as she could, listening for any sounds of Mitch moving around in the clinic. But the house was silent. Finally, she went to the door and stepped out into the hall. She had to talk to him. She had to get answers, and Mitch was the only one she could ask.

She turned to go to the front of the house, but she heard a muffled voice coming from the kitchen area and she turned. It sounded like Mitch talking to someone. She hesitated, not sure that she wanted to say anything in front of Doc. God knew he already thought she was having some difficulty with reality.

But the idea of going back into her room alone to wait some more wasn't very appealing. She'd go and see the men, then wait for a chance to talk to Mitch alone. She headed toward the kitchen, but when she got to the door, she realized that the voice wasn't coming from there. She turned and saw a short flight of steps leading down to a closed door.

The lab. Doc had said Mitch set it up in the partial basement. Slowly she went down the steps. When she got to the bottom, there was silence, then Mitch started talking again in a low, deep voice. She lifted her hand to knock, but lowered it, then touched the knob and quietly turned it. She decided to just look in, to make sure she wouldn't be interrupting some important discussion between the two men.

The door moved quietly back and she could see into a brightly lit room. Mitch sat on a wooden bench at a broad work table in the middle of the room. His shirt was gone, and she could see his bare arm and back, his broad shoulders. He was leaning forward a bit, his gray-streaked hair falling forward to partially hide his face. When he moved a bit, as if positioning himself better, she saw the muscles in his back and shoulders ripple with the effort.

Then Mitch lifted his head, and he was speaking, not to Doc, but as if he was recording what he was saying. He had something in his hand, something that flashed in the light as he moved it, and she heard him saying, "Since there are no control subjects available to me, the test will have to be on myself. I am going to make an incision next to the original injury, paralleling the path on the palm of my hand."

Harley watched in horror as he pressed a small sharp knife to his hand and started to cut an incision. "Oh, my God, no!" she gasped as blood began to ooze out of his hand.

Mitch jerked around when she spoke, and the knife slipped, slicing crookedly up to his wrist before it fell with a clatter to the metal tabletop. "What in the hell are you doing here?" he growled as he grabbed a white towel off the table and wrapped it around his hand.

"Mitch, my God, your hand! You cut it—you just cut it," she gasped as she moved farther into the glaringly lit room.

"You've got no right being in here," Mitch muttered as he slid off the stool. He held his injured hand against his chest and reached with the other one toward a video camera on the shelf. Then he turned on her. "What are you doing in here?"

"Me? You—you just cut yourself and..." She had to swallow at the sight of the blood oozing through the towel and smearing his naked chest. She held up a hand toward him. "Don't tell me I imagined that. My God, I'm not crazy. I'm not. You cut yourself."

"It's none of your business," he snapped as he came toward her, his cut hand pinned to his chest with his good one.

"Mitch, what's going on? How did that happen before? It just healed up, and I thought I was going mad, but now you...you know I'm not."

"All I know is you're interrupting," he said through clenched teeth.

"Interrupting you slicing your hand," she said. "I mean, you just cut it. Your hand—"

"Is none of your damned business."

She could feel the power of his anger, an anger that came out of nowhere and couldn't be accounted for by her walking in on him. The man she'd known for such a short time was gone, as if he had never been. Then she remembered that he'd been saying something when she looked in.

She pressed a hand to her mouth. "This—this is

a test of some sort?'' She looked at his hand wrapped in the bloody towel. "An experiment?"

He closed his eyes for a long moment, then opened them, and when he spoke, his voice was low and more controlled. "What did you hear?"

"Nothing. I mean, I heard you talking, but it didn't make any sense." She looked at his hands against his chest. "You sliced your hand open on purpose." She met his narrowed hazel eyes. "Why? Just tell me why this is all happening."

"I told you, it's none of your business."

"And your hand healing up before like that—that's none of my business either, is it?"

"You've got it."

"You just let me think I was hallucinating again. You let Doc think I was crazy! For God's sake, am I just supposed to pretend it didn't happen, that you didn't deliberately mutilate—"

"I made an incision," he muttered, "I didn't—"

His words were cut off as a convulsive tremor shook his body, then he groped behind him, his hand hitting the stool and sending it crashing sideways to the floor.

Harley instinctively reached out for Mitch, grabbing him by his arm, and she barely had time to register that his skin was ice-cold when he started to shake. She held tightly to his arm as he staggered back and leaned against the metal tabletop.

"What's wrong, Mitch? What's going on?" she asked.

He closed his eyes, and she could feel him start to pull free of her hand, but another spasm shook him. "Help...me to my room," he gasped.

She spotted an open door on the far side of the lab, and she could see a wood-paneled room through the opening. Slipping her arm around his waist, she tugged his good arm around her shoulders. "Lean on me," she said, and awkwardly helped him across the floor and into the next room.

Somehow she managed to get Mitch to the bed, and he sat on the sheets. As Harley eased her hold on him, he lay back against the light blue linen.

Harley looked down at him with his clenched jaw, closed eyes and his body shivering uncontrollably. "Mitch, tell me what to do for you. Where's Doc? I'll get him back here. Is there medicine I can get for you?"

He slowly moved his head from side to side. "No...not Doc...just..." When he shivered violently, Harley grabbed the comforter and pulled it up over him to his chin. She tucked it around him, but nothing seemed to be helping.

"What's happening to you?" she asked as she smoothed the hair back from his face with a shaky hand. "I don't know what to do."

"There's nothing...nothing." His voice was little more than a hoarse whisper. "Just...leave me...leave me alone."

She didn't even consider leaving. Instead, she turned and looked around, then saw a potbellied stove in one corner. She opened its door to find glowing embers in the bottom. Wood was stacked alongside it and she put some into the stove, then stirred it with a poker till it caught flame.

"I put more wood in the stove, Mitch," she told him when she returned to his side. His eyes were still closed and his breathing was ragged. Under the comforter his body was still trembling. She leaned closer to him. "Mitch, can you hear me?"

For one brief moment, his eyes opened and he looked at her, then they fluttered shut again. "I...I thought you'd gone," he rasped.

"I'm not leaving you like this," she said. "You need to get warm." As she touched his roughened face, his body shook with another tremor. "You need to get warm," she repeated, and did the only thing she could think to do.

She slipped under the comforter beside Mitch. His whole body was so cold it scared her. She lay next to him, facing him, then pulled the comforter up over both of them and put her arm around him. She could feel her own body being chilled by the cold, and she was startled when Mitch suddenly jerked back.

His right arm moved, the towel that had been

around the wound flying off and landing beyond the bed. "No, don't," he gasped. "Leave—"

"No," she said, and reached for him again.

He shivered convulsively, then with a low moan rolled away from her. "You can't..."

He wasn't in any shape to stop her, so she rolled with him, pressing herself along his back, angling her body to match his and putting her arm around his middle. All she had to give him was her warmth, and she wouldn't let him stop her from doing that.

She pressed her cheek to the cold smoothness of his back and closed her eyes tightly. For a moment, she had the strangest feeling that she was right where she belonged. Before she could figure out what was happening to her, the shivering grew more violent. And Harley held on to Mitch for dear life.

Chapter Nine

Mitch fought the chills as hard as he fought the
need to turn back to Harley and hold on to her. He
felt her heat against his back, the only heat in his
life at that moment. With no idea what was happening, he went with the trembling, curling more
tightly into a ball, and prayed to have it stop.

Gradually it did. The chill seemed to be dissolving, and the heat at his back felt as if it was invading his soul. It had been so long since he'd just let
go, since he'd felt a degree of relaxation, that he
barely recognized the sensation when it began to
envelop him. But just as it materialized, it began to
dissolve, pushed aside by the feel of Harley against
him.

He kept his eyes closed tightly, but couldn't
block out the sensations of her breasts against his
back, her hand on his skin and her leg over his
thighs. If he could have frozen a moment in time,

this would be it. He would have caught it in a bottle and saved it forever.

Just when he was starting to believe it was over, the cold came back. The shivering returned with a vengeance, and he shook uncontrollably. For a shattering instant, he could feel himself slipping away, going to a darkness that was waiting for him, almost beckoning him. Grayness was creeping up, and he knew if it kept coming, he'd be smothered by it.

Then something happened. Harley held him, her arm around his waist, her hand pressed to his middle, and her voice was everywhere, mingling with a heat that he could almost feel. "Mitch, it's okay," she whispered. "I'm here." And it was as if Harley was pulling him back from the darkness, away from the cold and fear. She was his anchor, his shelter, and the shivering stopped.

The focus of everything in his being was her, holding on to him, and the heat she was giving him. He was safe. He had her against him. When her hand moved on him, gently stroking his abdomen, he trembled, but it had nothing to do with what he'd just been through.

Her softness was heartbreaking and her gentleness almost more than he could bear. Then her palm was on his arm, stroking him from his shoulder to his hand, clenched on his thigh.

Another pain came to him. He was so close to her, yet he couldn't turn and do the one thing he wanted more than anything right then—to just hold her. He wanted to feel her against him and lose himself in the scent of her, to know her touch on him and to never let go.

As that thought materialized, a part of him wished she'd disappeared, that he'd never known that feeling of her body at his back. Yet another part was terrified that she'd leave and he'd be totally alone again.

"It's okay," she whispered, the heat of her breath caressing his shoulder so seductively that he could feel it coursing through his body. "It's okay."

He wished that was true. He couldn't move as her hand shifted to his back, running lightly over his shoulder blade and down to his waist. As she slipped her arm around his waist again, he muttered hoarsely, "It's over. It's over."

He heard her sigh, a shuddering sound that vibrated along his back. "Thank goodness."

"Yes," he said. He tried to move away from her but he was stopped by something remarkable—he felt weak. It was a sensation he hadn't experienced since injecting himself with the serum. And he knew that he was entering into another phase. The spontaneous healing, the cold, now this.

Then he realized that if he was weak, he couldn't hurt her. He shifted onto his back, and he drew in a deep shuddering breath when he saw Harley right there, on her side, supporting herself on one elbow and looking down at him with those blue eyes.

He cautiously reached out with one hand, making contact with her shoulder. The reality of her under his fingers raced through him, soft and warm. Then he trailed his fingers to her throat, to the pulse he'd felt there when he'd found her in the car. Instead of a vague fluttering, her pulse beat quickly and surely.

"Lady, I..." His words were lost when she shifted closer to him. All he could do was drink in the vision of her: the way her hair fell softly around her face; the swelling of her breasts under the thin cotton of her shirt. He lifted his hand to her cheek, to silky skin, then he eased his hand under her hair, cupping her neck.

He'd never felt anything like her. Nothing this soft, this silky, this alive. He felt his chest tighten and his body respond on such a basic level that it was almost painful for him.

When her tongue touched her slightly parted lips, he felt the tension grow—a tension that he'd come to fear since taking the serum. He could feel his muscles tightening, and he jerked his hand back, knowing it had been too good to last that he could touch her without fear. He'd been a fool. He turned from her and stared up at the heavy beams of the ceiling. "Thanks for helping," he said, his voice no more than a rasping whisper.

When her fingers touched his jaw and gently urged him to look at her, he fought the pressure until she drew back. He thought she was leaving, and he braced himself for the emptiness. But he was wrong, as wrong as he'd been in thinking he could trust himself to touch her.

She didn't leave. Instead, she came so close that he felt the warmth of her breath on his face. "Mitch, what's happening?"

He stared hard at the ceiling. There were no words left in him, not even lies. So he kept silent.

It startled him when he felt her move again. This time she put one arm over him, bracing it by his right shoulder. Then she levered herself above him. She was right in front of his face, and there was nowhere to look but into her incredible blue eyes. Her loose hair fell around them, forming a dark curtain that included just the two of them in its protection. It closed off the world and everything of no consequence right then.

She looked at him for what seemed forever, then slowly came to him, and her lips found his. His whole being was more alive in that moment than at any other time in his life. Her shirt brushed his bare chest, her thighs were against his and her hair tickled his shoulders.

Her lips were soft and inviting, touching him with gentle heat. And in some indefinable way, he knew that he'd been waiting for this moment all his life. He was alive because of Harley. Because she held him and warmed him and pulled him back to her.

When her lips teased his, when her tongue ran over his teeth, he could feel his body responding again, that tension coming in a burst of white-hot force, and he clenched his hands around the cotton of the comforter. Her taste invaded him, and his hands ached, an ache echoed in his body, which had a fiery need of its own.

Just when he didn't think he could bear it any longer, she was moving back, but not leaving him. When he opened his eyes, she was still over him, so close her essence filled him. A hunger that knew no bounds consumed him and he fought it with every atom of his being.

"Mitch," she breathed, her own voice hoarse with the desire that echoed in him. "I—I..." Her tongue touched her softly parted lips, and it drove him mad with desire. All he wanted was to pull her back to him and know her completely.

But all he could do was lie there, his ragged breathing echoing around him, his body tight and uncomfortable in his jeans. Cursing fate, or whatever it was that controlled what happened, wouldn't do any good. He had only himself to blame for this mess. That last thought almost ripped open his heart. It was his fault that he could never love Harley. And the tension increased.

Harley gazed down at Mitch. She'd been so certain that he wanted her as much as she wanted him—how could she have been so wrong? He hadn't responded to her at all, and she felt foolish and adolescent. To impulsively kiss him like that just because he touched her in gratitude, to as good as invite him to make love to her, was the most foolish thing she'd ever done. Embarrassment was painful, and she rolled off the bed to stand on the cold floor with her back to him.

"Boy, I'm...sorry about that." She hugged her arms around herself, missing the feel of him against her. "I just...it's been so crazy."

There was no response behind her, and she was ready to walk out the door and never look back when she heard the bedsprings creak and felt Mitch brush lightly against her arm.

The next thing she knew, he was standing within inches of her. She could still see the effects of whatever had happened to him stamped on his face. Tension had cut deep lines at his mouth and between his eyes, and she didn't miss the way he reached for the footboard and held it for support.

Then she glanced down, away from the narrowed hazel eyes, and she knew that the desire hadn't been entirely one-sided. There was physical evidence that he'd been aroused. But that didn't mean he wanted to make love with her. She looked back up to his face.

"You should stay in bed," she said. "You…need to rest. And I'm sorry."

With a rasping sigh, he raked his fingers roughly through his thick hair, brushing it back from his face. "I don't need to rest," he said in a deep tone. "And I don't want your apology."

What Harley needed was to be out of there and away from a man who could arouse her just by his nearness. "That was probably the aftereffects of what's happened. That's what Doc said. My body chemistry isn't just right and…" She couldn't finish that sentence. It was so obviously a lie. She couldn't blame what she'd done on chemicals. Hormones, yes, but not a chemical imbalance. "Then I was worried about you. You were so sick. I…think I need to try and find Doc and—"

"No," he said quickly. "I don't want Doc knowing anything about this."

"But Doc—"

"Trust me on this and promise me you won't mention it to him. He'd just worry, and he doesn't need that."

She hesitated, then moved a bit closer and impulsively touched his right hand, which was hanging by his side. He flinched slightly at the contact, but didn't fight her when she lifted his hand and turned it palm up. She wasn't shocked when she saw that the original wound was almost invisible now, and the one he'd inflicted on himself was closed and barely raw. Somehow she'd expected that.

A miracle—and she expected it of the man. She touched the new wound with her finger and felt him tense at the contact, then she looked up at him. "Tell me about this. Tell me I'm not going crazy. Tell me what's happening."

He pulled back from her, closing his hand tightly before pushing it behind his back. "You're not crazy, but it's nothing to do with you."

Suddenly an anger burned in her. "Nothing to do with me? I see you cut yourself, then you almost..." She swallowed hard, not able to finish that statement. "I'm the one who felt you get so cold, the one who was there when you were shaking so badly you couldn't stand up. Don't tell me it's nothing to do with me. I'm right in the middle of this and I don't have a clue what it's all about. You owe me."

"I don't owe you. We're even. The score card's at a draw, and let's leave it that way."

"It's not even close to a draw," she said, standing her ground.

"Lady, why don't you just give up?"

She couldn't explain that to him, because she couldn't explain it to herself. "I just want to know."

He turned from her as if she hadn't spoken, and crossed to the woodstove. She could tell he was a bit unsteady on his feet, but the weakness she'd sensed in him right after the episode seemed to be leaving. He reached for the poker, then opened the door of the stove and silently stirred the glowing wood until there were flames again.

When he finally stood back and put the poker in the holder, Harley felt as if she was going to scream. But she managed to speak in a reasonable voice. "Mitch, if you don't tell me, I'll have to tell Doc."

He cast her a look over his shoulder. "What?"

"Explain this to me and I'll keep silent. I won't tell anyone."

"I don't like blackmail."

That word rocked her. "I don't, either."

"Then walk out that door and leave it alone."

She knew it was probably the smart thing to do, but she couldn't. She stood where she was and hugged herself more tightly, her fingers pressing into her upper arms. "I'm not leaving."

"God, you're stubborn."

"I thought we went through all of this before."

He ran a hand roughly over his face, then exhaled with a low hiss. "I can't tell you. You could never understand what it's like to have something in your life that could destroy you and everyone around you." He shook his head, his expression bleak. "No one knows what damage the truth can do."

"I know what it's like," she blurted out. "I know."

He narrowed his eyes. "Sure, you know what it's like. You know what it is to be so afraid of people knowing the truth about you that you can't sleep, you can't eat, you think of ending your own life."

She flinched at his words, words that described her frame of mind since Freeman had come back into her life. "So afraid that you'll lose everything and everyone that matters?" she asked in a low, unsteady voice. "Oh, I know, Mitch, I know exactly what you're talking about."

"Don't lie to me," he muttered. "Don't do this."

"Oh, I've lied in the past, but I'm not lying now."

He moved slowly to the desk, set under a series of high windows on the side wall. He grabbed the straight-backed chair, turned it around, then sat down on it, facing her.

She could see him rest his hands palms down on his thighs, and his fingers pressed into the denim. "So, you have a secret?" he finally asked.

She kept the distance between them, because if she went closer to him, she knew she'd touch him. She'd hold him and not let go. No man had ever turned her emotions on and off the way he did, and right now those emotions were raw and painful. She knew the time for lying and hiding was over. "Yes,

I have a secret. And if it gets out, I'll lose everything. These past eight years won't mean a thing.''

He stared at her silently for a very long moment,
his eyes narrowing on her as he slowly rubbed his
hands on his thighs. ''Tell me about it,'' he finally
said.

''If you tell me about what's happening to you.''
He studied her intently, those hazel eyes losing
none of their intensity despite what he'd just been
through. ''Well?'' she asked when she was about
to scream from the strained silence.

''I'm just trying to figure out what you could tell
me about yourself that you wouldn't want anyone
to know.''

''Will you tell me?''

He sat back in the chair and rested his head
against the high back. His eyes were hooded, the
lids partially closed, and she could see a pulse beating slowly and strongly in his throat. ''Okay.''

''And I can trust you?''

He almost smiled, but the expression only shadowed his lips, then was gone. ''Quit while you're
ahead.''

She stayed where she was by the bed and spoke
quickly, to get it out before she chickened out on
the deal.

''My name's Harley Madison and I'm from Los
Angeles. And I never forgot that.''

A frown tugged a line between his eyes. "What do you mean?"

"I never had amnesia." She could barely look at him while she spoke. "I thought you and Doc might recognize me, and I couldn't chance that."

"Recognize you? What in the hell—"

She cut him off. "I agree it sounds silly now that I know the two of you, but I've been in magazines and newspapers, in commercials and on bill-boards." She shrugged. "Not that you and Doc seem like the kind to read glamour magazines or anything."

"Lady, if you think this is earth-shattering for someone not to recognize you, I've got news for you."

"Eight years ago, when I came to Los Angeles from a little town in Texas, I was going to make it big. I never went to college, never had the money to, and the best I could do was waitressing. But I'd had people tell me that I had a look, that I should be a model, and I took them seriously. So I headed out to Los Angeles with two hundred dollars in my pocket and the foolish idea that one more pretty face in Los Angeles would get noticed."

Mitch shifted forward in the chair and rested his forearms on his thighs as she spoke. "Is there some deep dark secret hidden in this rags-to-riches story?"

She took a shaky breath, then blurted it out. "Eight years ago I was arrested for prostitution."

That brought his head up with a start, and she could see the shock on his face. "What?"

"Prostitution, or maybe it was solicitation. I can't remember now, but I was arrested. I wasn't— I mean, I didn't..." She didn't miss the way he was eyeing her, as if he was wondering just who he was looking at. "I'm not," she said. "I never have. I answered an ad for this agency when I first hit town, and I went in to interview, and I met with a guy named Freeman Diaz. He said he was an agent and that I had 'the look' he was searching for, and he wanted me to work for the agency. So I signed on. I was at the agency getting my pictures taken when the police burst in. It was a raid."

She touched her tongue to her lips. "Obviously it was an escort service, and the modeling was a front. I was too stupid to know it, and I believed Freeman. They let me go after one long night in jail, and I went back to waiting on tables for two years until I found a terrific agent who believed in me and helped me start a career."

When Harley stopped speaking, there was silence in the room for a long, nerve-racking moment. Until it was broken by his voice. "And this is your secret—that you aren't a prostitute?"

"Yes. Well, no, it's just I don't want it to get out. It could do all sorts of harm. I've got this new contract that's being negotiated, and this could kill it."

"Why would they ever know? It's been eight years."

"Freeman contacted me a few days ago, and he wants part of the action or he's going to go public with it. He'll sell the story to the highest bidder and I'll lose everything. Tara Gaye Cosmetics wants me for a campaign called the American Dream." She shook her head. "I can see the headlines now—The American Dream Hooker."

"You're being blackmailed," he said, not a question, just a low statement.

"Threatened. Freeman thinks I owe him. He wants me to sign a contract on Monday that gives him part of everything I make." She could feel her hands tightening painfully. "He laughed and said that if I didn't do it, he'd destroy me. He'd take away everything I've worked for and struggled for and laugh while he did it. I wanted to kill him. I mean, I had a gun and…"

"You tried to—"

"Oh, no, I didn't. I just thought about it. I left town. I had to get out of there, and I was just driving and driving until I knew what I was going to do. Then I was here and there was the accident."

His expression tightened as she spoke, then he cleared his throat. "This contract and your life, the way it is—they're that important to you that you were going to kill the guy?"

She almost said they were the most important things in her life, but suddenly that sounded so shallow and wrong to her. "They're important, but I wasn't going to kill for them. I just thought about it. Tara Gaye's people are talking about a five-year contract, and the money..." She shrugged sharply. "It's the biggest thing in my career."

"Ah, now we get to the root of all evil," he said as he eyed her intently. "Money."

"I grew up poor, and now that I'm finally at a stage where I can be comfortable, I don't want to lose it. No one would. Why would I want to go back to scrimping and saving and working tables? And Freeman can do that to me. Freeman *will* do that to me if I don't go along with him."

"So, if you give in to the guy, he keeps quiet and keeps on sucking you dry?"

"Pretty much," she murmured.

"Lady, your worries are just starting if you fall for that garbage. He drains off money, you have to explain that to your agent, and what's to say that someone else isn't sitting out there waiting to do what old Freeman's already doing to you? Do you go through life just shooting people when they show up?"

Harley's head was starting to hurt as she realized how stupid she'd been to think this was a simple matter of giving in to Freeman. She leaned back against the bed, her legs decidedly wobbly. "Oh, God," she whispered. "Things were so good, then they just collapsed. Like a house of cards."

He stood and slowly walked over to her. He

looked down at her and said, "I'll concede that your secret is one that could really ruin you, but do you want some advice?"

Despite the fact they were talking about life-and-death matters, she was distracted by the way Mitch was tucking his hair behind his ears. His hand was healed almost completely now, and she could tell he was regaining his strength rapidly. "What sort of advice?" she asked.

"For what it's worth, I'd go with the truth. Beat that creep to the punch. Go public yourself. Tell everyone that you didn't know what this agency was doing. You wouldn't have been there if you had, and you were released when the cops realized that you hadn't done anything wrong."

"What if it blows up in my face?"

"Life doesn't hand out guarantees. And there are a lot worse things than waiting on tables, believe me."

"You don't understand."

"Oh, lady, I understand all too well. You make a dumb choice, a choice you can't back out of, then it comes back and hits you in the face when you least expect it."

With that, he turned from her. He reached for the poker and pushed at the smoldering logs till they shot sparks and took flame again.

When he finally turned back to Harley, his expression was devoid of the emotion she'd just seen there. He'd shut down again. She shifted nervously, remembering the kitchen, when she'd seen his shock. Then he'd banished it as if it had never been.

In a voice that matched his expression Mitch said, "I made a choice once. A stupid choice." He lifted one eyebrow. "It makes yours look like a walk in the park."

"What are you talking about?"

He tucked the tips of his fingers in the pockets of his jeans and rocked forward on the balls of his feet. "My secret—life and death—because of a bad choice I made."

She studied him and asked a question she hated to ask. "You're sick?"

"In a way. But not like any sickness you'd understand." He grabbed a T-shirt from a dresser drawer and took his time putting it on. With quick, sharp strokes he tucked it into the waistband of his jeans and then looked back at her.

"Sit down," he said.

She slid back on the bed and Mitch came over to her, standing two feet from her. He didn't touch her, but she was vividly aware of his closeness and the feeling that even though she'd asked him to tell her, she wasn't at all sure she wanted to know his secret now.

"Okay, you asked for it. This is all a test, a month-long test. And all I've found out is I've created a monster. I'm the monster."

Chapter Ten

Before Harley could stop him, Mitch began talking in a low, rough voice, one all but devoid of emotion. And his eyes never left her face. He told her about some research he'd been doing, looking for something to aid people who had to undergo prolonged surgery. A medication that would help weakened bodies survive invasive procedures that would normally kill them.

He told her about his serum, about testing it, then asking for a go-ahead to use human subjects. She didn't understand some of what he was saying, but when he told her about getting drunk, about injecting himself with the serum, she understood that with painful clarity.

"You injected yourself?" she asked, the first time she'd spoken since he started his explanation.

He nodded. "I was drunk, angry, and I don't remember doing it, but I did."

"But you're okay, so it wasn't too bad. I mean, you're here."

"Yes, I'm here, because I can't be anywhere else. Only one person knows what I'm going to tell you now, and it's not Doc. His name is Luke Stewart. He works with me at the lab and he's backing me up on this. He's at the lab now, working on that end. And I'm here."

She pressed her hands to her thighs. "This seizure, or whatever it is that you had. It's because of that serum, isn't it? And your hand, healing like that?"

"I think so. That's why I'm here, trying to figure out just what I've done to myself."

"What *have* you done to yourself?" she whispered.

"Created a monster," he growled with cutting passion and pain deep in his eyes. Whatever emotion he'd been reining in was unleashed. "A monster who needs no sleep, has unending endurance, strength beyond any normal man's strength, speed without stress on the body. And now spontaneous healing."

She listened in stunned silence, till the truth was out. The unbelievable truth. She wasn't crazy or imagining things. "It was you," she gasped. "You turned the car over and tore off the door." She slipped off the bed and stood right in front of him, feeling as if the world was tipping precariously off balance for her. "Mitch, you can fly?"

He ran a hand roughly over his face. "No, I can't fly, but I can run fast."

"Superman," she whispered.

"Far from it. But I have my kryptonite."

"The shivering and the cold?"

"And blackouts. I lose time and I have no idea where I've been or what I've done. And I don't know why it's happening. I can't find a link." He looked down at his own hands. "Spontaneous healing, but at what price?"

"Price?"

He cast her a shadowed glance. "Think of the possibilities. Invincible armies. World domination by simply sending out armies of men injected with the serum. You wouldn't need bombs or destructive nuclear weapons. Just men."

"Armies that can heal themselves," she whispered in amazement as his words sank in.

"Exactly."

"It doesn't wear off?"

"It hasn't, until..." He shook his head sharply. "I've hardly needed sleep during this time, but right after that spell, I was weak and I—" He broke off and flexed his shoulders. "But that's gone now."

"And Doc doesn't know anything about it?"

"No, he's sticking to our deal. No questions, and

he gets the lab when I leave. He's a good man and he's held up his end of the bargain.''

''And what's going to happen now?''

''You're going to keep quiet about all of this, and I'll see it out to the end.'' He hesitated. ''I'm finding out new things all the time. So you see that secrecy is vital?''

''Yes, of course. What do you think is going to happen?''

''I have no idea.'' He turned back to the stove and crouched by the hearth, picking up the poker he'd laid by it to prod at the burning embers. Sparks shot up the chimney with each poke, but the flames were all but gone. ''And I have no one to blame but myself.''

''This Luke Stewart—what about him?''

''The program's been put on hold and the lab thinks I've taken a sabbatical. Luke's doing some tests for me, watching the lab subjects.''

''You've got strength and endurance and healing. It seems that your experiment is more than what you hoped for.''

She didn't understand when he laughed, a harsh, humorless sound. ''I've got endurance, but can't sleep. I've got speed, but I've got blackouts, and I have strength, but...'' He shook his head sharply. ''It's *much* more than I hoped for. It's devastating.''

''Mitch, it can't be that bad. Your hand's all better. And you're okay now.''

He stood abruptly and turned to her with the poker in his hands, his expression tight and almost pained. "I've turned myself into a man who isn't a man. A man who doesn't know what is going to happen, and who can't touch even the simplest things and enjoy them."

"What do you mean?"

He crossed to her. "Touching. Just the simple act of holding something..." His eyes narrowed, and she hardly heard him whisper, "Or someone."

"I don't—"

"If I don't concentrate every minute, if I forget just for a second, whatever I'm touching could be crushed."

"But I saw you touch things."

"Like the glass that broke?"

"That was an accident. It broke. It had to have had a flaw—"

Her words were cut off when he lifted the poker and handed it to her. "This is what I mean," he said.

Cautiously she took the implement, not understanding. The metal still held heat from the fire as she touched it. Then she looked down and saw ridges along the solid metal shaft, ridges that hadn't been forged there. She ran her finger over them, then knew the truth. They were a finger pattern. From a large hand. Mitch had pressed the hard metal as if it were butter.

"You—you couldn't," she breathed, holding the poker as if it were a poisonous snake.

"But I did," he said, taking the poker from her. "My touch, my power. And that's when I'm controlling it. Now you understand."

"I can't believe it," she said, but she did. And now she believed the bent rail on the bed. It was true, but she protested one more time. "It can't be."

"It is." Mitch put the poker in its holder on the wall. "Believe it."

She stared at him, at his back, the way the muscles in his shoulders worked under the thin cotton of the T-shirt as he clenched his hands. A need to take away the pain she could see in his stance drove her to cross the room to him, and without even thinking, she slipped her hands around his waist. She pressed her cheek to his back, to the reassuring heat there, and shut out the way his breath caught at her touch.

"Oh, Mitch, it's going to be all right. It has to be."

"Don't." He breathed unsteadily, his voice echoing all around her. "Don't touch me."

But the need was so powerful she didn't even think about doing what he said. She hooked her arms upward, around his shoulders, and didn't let go. "It's going to be all right."

Mitch groaned, a low, almost animalistic sound,

then he turned sharply away from her. She felt her hands lose their grip on him, then they were empty and he was facing her.

She looked into a face etched with pain, and she could tell his breathing was ragged. "I can't do this," he muttered through clenched teeth. "I can't."

Mitch felt as if his body had been branded by Harley's touch. He could almost feel the imprint of her hands on his stomach, then on his shoulders. And his need to take that touch and keep it with him forever was cut off by the cold hard fact that forever was something he had no investment in. Minute to minute, hour to hour, day to day—that was as far as he could look, and he had to go through it alone.

His breathing was rapid, but not from exertion. Somehow, the pain in him was speeding up his respiration, and he had to take a couple of deep, cleansing breaths before he could talk. "Touching." He shook his head. "I can't. You saw the poker. I can't."

Her blue eyes were overly bright, and he didn't miss the way she was nervously lacing her hands together. "But you touched me...on the bed. You touched me."

He closed his eyes, needing to block out the sight of her so he could think straight. "I was weak from the seizure, but that's over." He opened his eyes and deliberately looked past her. "I could hurt you. God help me, I would hurt you."

"No, you wouldn't," she said in a touchingly shaky voice.

Then he did look at her, and wished he hadn't. Deep in the blue depths of her eyes, he saw trust, and God help him, he couldn't let her be that foolish. So he said words that he prayed would keep her away from him.

"I have hurt you, over and over again."

"No, you—"

"I have," he insisted. "That flash on the road before you crashed. It was me. I was out running. I don't remember anything, but I was there. And when I rescued you, I bruised your arms where I held you. Don't you understand? If I could concentrate and be focused, I could touch anything. But, lady, that's impossible with you around."

He'd said she was stubborn, he just didn't know how stubborn until she moved. Her hand was on him before he knew what was happening, pressed to his chest over his heart. "It's not impossible," she whispered.

He looked down into her upturned face, the need in him to take her there and then a burning, living thing. "Don't touch me," he groaned. "Because if you do, I'll take you, and I could kill you."

Her hand jerked back as if he'd burned her, and the irony of getting what he wanted, then having it tear at his heart, wasn't lost on him. That trust was dimming, and fear was creeping into the depths of her eyes. He hated himself at that moment more than he had ever hated anything in his life. But he took that chance and moved away from her to the bed.

It took all of his willpower to speak then, to say words that he knew he had to say. "I don't want you here."

"But I could help."

He gripped the footboard of the bed and closed his eyes. "You can't help yourself, so how could you help me?"

There was silence, then she spoke. "We'll talk about this later, won't we?"

"Sure," he lied.

"You know Doc would help, don't you?"

"I care too much about him to drag him into this." *And I care too much for you,* he thought, but never said the words. He didn't want to care about anyone, but he knew it was too late to stop now.

He felt her move away from him, and as she left the room, he could feel the emptiness flooding back into the spaces where she'd been. Aching emptiness that he knew was just the start of a torment being inflicted on him all because of a woman with blue eyes and a stubborn streak that would put a mule to shame.

He turned from the room he'd looked on as a

sanctuary since coming here, but now seemed like a tomb. Quickly, he went out into the lab, where there wasn't a feeling that all he had to do was look up and see Harley there. And there wasn't a huge bed where she'd held him.

HARLEY BARELY KNEW how to react to anything that had happened that night. She went back to her room, but sleep wouldn't come. Every time she closed her eyes, she saw Mitch. Every time she moved, she could feel him by her, and she finally got out of bed just before dawn and was about to go to the bathroom when she glanced out the window.

There in the half-light of the new day, with the land silvered and gray, she saw Mitch. He stood in the clearing, his hands at his sides, his head thrown back as if studying the lightening sky. She halfway expected him to sense her at the window, but he never turned. He shook his head, then looked toward the woods, and suddenly he was gone. She could see the tracks his feet had cut through the snow, dark holes in the pristine whiteness, but Mitch was nowhere in sight.

Harley stood at the window for what seemed forever, staring at the deeply shadowed trees, and it took her off guard to realize that she was crying. Silent, hot tears slid down her face, tears that hadn't come the night before. And she had no real idea why she was crying.

She swiped at her eyes, then knew what she was going to do. Quickly she dressed, then put on her heavy jacket and boots and went through the dark clinic to the back door. She stepped out into cutting cold, where the sky was streaked with pinks and yellows as the sun started to rise. Without looking back, she went through the snow, following Mitch's footprints.

She didn't know what she was going to do or say when she found him, but she knew that she had to find him. Trudging through the heavy snow, she went into the woods, watching Mitch's footprints carefully. They were becoming smudged and angled, as if made by someone running quickly. But she could barely lift her feet to step in them.

The air was so cold it almost burned as she breathed it in, and she pushed her hands deeply in her pockets to try and keep them warm. Just when she was about to go back, she saw light ahead, and stepped out into a small clearing. The woods fell away on one side, opening to a spectacular view from the top of a ridge across a deep gorge and up to mountains that were etched starkly by the rising sun.

At the very edge of the drop-off, she saw Mitch sitting motionless on a huge rock, staring out into the distance. Harley made her way across the snow, and when she got close to him, she could see that his watch cap was pulled low and his eyes were closed tightly.

"Mitch?" she said as she got to the rock and near the edge of the drop-off. "Mitch?"

He jerked around, and she was pinned by hazel eyes that looked stunned. They blinked quickly, then he ran a hand roughly over his face. "What…?" He looked away from her to the surrounding land, then back at Harley. "What's going on?"

Harley got closer, close enough to see the strain in his mouth and eyes. "I saw you leave and I came after you. You shouldn't be out in this weather, not after what happened. Why are you out here?"

"I don't know," he said in a voice so low she almost couldn't hear it. "I…" He shook his head sharply and looked away to the view again. He was silent for a long moment, then spoke in a low, rough voice. "I don't know. I was in the lab, working, then I'm here." His chuckle was harsh and uncomfortable. "Bingo, magic…insanity."

"Mitch, don't."

"Oh, God," he said with a labored sigh. "I lost time again. Just one more glitch in this mess. And I ended up here."

She went closer and had to fight the urge to reach out and touch him. "Mitch, you need to see someone. That friend of yours—he might be able to help.''

Mitch exhaled roughly, the warmth of his breath curling into the air. "No, there's nothing that can be done. I just have to wait to see where this all leads...eventually.''

"You can't do it alone.''

"Why not?'' He cast her a sideways glance before looking back into the distance. "I've done everything on my own all my life.''

"What happened to your parents?'' she asked, wanting to understand him just a bit.

He shrugged, the action tugging at the heavy jacket across his shoulders. "The only things I know I've been told. I have no memories of them. They're both dead, and I was brought here when I was three or four. I was here until I got a scholarship to premed school, and I haven't been back...until now.''

"It's your home.''

"You know when Doc and his wife were running this place, they had twenty kids at a time. There must have been hundreds of kids passing through here over the years, but Doc told me that no one has ever come back...except me.''

"I can tell he's glad to have you here.''

"He thinks I'll agree to take over his practice and keep this place going. I've tried to tell him that's not in the cards, but he doesn't give up.'' He cast her a slanting glance. "He's a lot like you in the stubborn department."

"Maybe, if things change, you could—"

"They won't change, at least not for the good. And Doc needs someone here who'll love doing it the way he does. That's not me."

"What if this hadn't happened, if you came back just to visit and he asked you? What then?"

"What if?" he whispered, then shook his head sharply. "I can't deal in what-ifs."

She shivered at the chilly wind starting to kick up as the sun crested over the trees. "I think we need to get back. It's so cold out here and Doc's going to be back and wonder where we are."

Mitch motioned her off with one hand. "You go back. I'll be along later."

"Mitch…?"

He turned to her again, his eyes blurred by the morning light. "Lady, don't look at me like that."

"Like what?"

He stood and walked precariously close to the edge of the ravine as he crossed the snowy ground to where she stood. He seemed overly large in the heavy outdoor clothes and it was hard to believe he'd been so helpless last night. "Like that," he murmured. "Damn it, I can't take that."

"I don't understand."

He eyed her for a long moment, then turned back

to the view and the ever-brightening sun. "Understand this—I don't have anything for you."

"I didn't ask for anything," she said, closing her fingers over the thick sleeve of his jacket. "I don't want anything from you."

He closed his eyes for a moment, then exhaled, the vapor of his breath rising into the skies and disappearing almost as soon as it formed.

He turned abruptly to her, inches separating them, then his hands rose, and for a moment she thought he was going to capture her face between them. "That makes you a hell of a lot different from me." But there was no contact. They stopped just inches away, so close she could feel his heat radiating against her cheeks.

He stood very still, his breathing ragged, then slowly she pulled his hands to her. As he touched her cheeks, the contact was almost searing. Time seemed to freeze in place. There was no coldness, no isolation, just she and Mitch, joined in some way she couldn't begin to fathom.

But before she could do anything else, a sound tore from him that was akin to a cry of pain in a wounded animal, and his hands jerked back from hers. He spun away from her, stumbling to the rock. He plunged his hands into the blanketing snow, then leaned forward, his shoulders hunched, and she could hear him taking rapid, ragged breaths.

"My God," he said in a shaky voice. "I can't.

Don't you understand? I can't. God help me, I want to. I want to touch you and..." He took a sharp breath that made his whole being shake, then he exhaled and said in a rough whisper, "God help me."

This man, almost a stranger to her, touched her in a way that she'd never known before. She felt his pain as if it were her own, and it mingled in her with a helplessness that almost choked her.

"Mitch—"

Without warning, he spun around, and there was a rage in his face that startled her. "Just get out of here. Get away from me."

She felt tears burn her eyes, but she didn't go. She stood her ground, then slowly went to him, put her arms around him, and while he stood absolutely still, she held him. Something in her wouldn't let her let go, and she almost felt the way she had the night before—that she was keeping him from going somewhere horrible and frightening. A place she could feel herself slipping toward at the thought of leaving him alone.

"Harley, please..."

"Just hold me," she whispered.

She felt his whole being shudder with a pain she could feel stab her soul, but she didn't let go.

Mitch dared not move. If he did, he'd hold Harley to him and never let her go. And he couldn't do that.

"Mitch, Mitch," he heard her saying, but he couldn't even look at her. The coldness of the early morning cut through him, but not from the wind and the snow. It was a cold born out of denial and isolation. A cold that he could almost taste as he turned and headed away from the only warmth in his world.

He moved quickly, heading back to the house, intent on getting to a phone to find some way to get her out of this place as soon as possible. When he broke into the clearing at the back of the clinic, he didn't have to look to know Harley wasn't behind him. The emptiness was complete and as horrific as it had been in his room the night before, but he couldn't go back.

He hurried into the house and called out, "Doc? Are you here?"

"In here, Mitch."

He went to the front of the house and into Doc's office, near the reception area. Doc was sitting behind his desk, looking very old and very tired. This was getting to be too much for him, and Mitch had a "what-if"—what if things were different, what if he could stay? He knew then that he would have stayed. But that was just as impossible as everything seemed right now.

"What's going on, son?" Doc asked as Mitch went into the office.

"Just out for a while." He took off his jacket

and dropped it on a table by the door before he sat in the chair facing the desk. "I came back to see if you were here. How's the Fisher kid doing?"

"She's just fine. Actually, she was fine last night, but her mother was a basket case. They lost a boy about three years ago, a skiing accident, and she overreacts to this sort of thing. I wanted to keep an eye on her, too." He patted his stomach. "And she's one hell of a cook."

"Doc, how easy is it to get out of here now?"

"*Easy* is a relative word. With a four-by-four, you can make it. Why?"

"Harley needs to get back to Los Angeles, and she needs a car. I was hoping you might be able to take her down to Dumbarton and get a car for her there."

"What about her things in the wreck? Were you able to get to them?"

"Not yet, but I will."

"Okay. I need to check on a couple of patients, and this evening I've been asked to the Haydens' place. They wanted you to come, too. You remember Genna Hayden? Her mother used to help out here in the summers."

Mitch had a vague memory of her, but shook his head. "Thank them, but I've got work to do. When will you be able to get her to Dumbarton?"

"Tomorrow morning first thing. We can call ahead for a car, then get her down there. Or you could run her down there today, if she's in a big hurry.''

Mitch couldn't trust himself to drive. "No, tomorrow morning's good." He could stay in the lab and work until then. "Could you call for a rental car for her?"

"Sure, then I'm heading out for the house calls. Want to come along?"

"No, not this time."

The old man didn't fight him on it. He just nodded. "Okay, I'll be back later on. If there's an emergency, page me."

"Sure," Mitch said, then crossed to get his coat and head toward the back of the house. He was almost at the stairs to the lab when he heard a door open and close, then footsteps on the wooden floor. He stopped and waited, then Harley was there.

Chapter Eleven

Her face was flushed from the cold and the exertion, and as she skimmed back the hood on her jacket, Mitch felt his breath catch at the clear beauty she possessed.

An ache that had been there for what seemed forever intensified uncomfortably when she spoke in a slightly breathless voice. "It's a long walk back." She studied him with wide blue eyes, but before she could say anything else, Doc came up behind Mitch.

"Well, hello there. I was wondering where you got to." As she began to unbutton her coat, he said, "Mitch just got back from a walk. It's too bad you didn't go with him. He knows the area around here like the back of his hand."

"I'm sure he didn't want company," she murmured, and Mitch didn't miss the way she was clasping her hands together, so tightly that the knuckles were white.

"How're you feeling?" Doc asked.

"Much better, thank you."

"Mitch said you wanted to leave as soon as possible."

She darted a quick look at Mitch, and he could see the way she clenched her jaw. But she said with reasonable calmness, "Yes, I do."

Mitch couldn't stand there with her so close, and the air in the house was getting thin for him. "I'm just heading out to where you had the accident. I'll get your things for you, then you can leave first thing in the morning."

Doc picked up the plan. "I'll run you down to Dumbarton in the morning to get a rental car. I got a reservation for you all set."

"I'd appreciate that."

"I'm off on rounds, and since Mitch is going out again, could you do me a favor?"

"Anything."

"If the phone rings, answer it, and if it's an emergency, my pager number is right by the phone in my office. Page me, okay?"

"I will."

"That's great. My office is the room right near the front door. Now, I need to change, then get out there." Mitch felt him pat him once on the shoulder. "You two keep warm, and I'll see you tonight. I shouldn't be too late, and with any luck, I won't get any emergencies." He left them to go to his room.

Mitch didn't move. He didn't trust himself to move and not go to Harley. Instead he said, "I'm leaving, too."

"Well, I guess you don't need a key to get into my Jeep, do you?"

Mitch wondered if she was making a joke, but there was no humor in her face. "I'll be back in an hour or so."

"Sure," she whispered, then passed him to go to her room.

For a moment the air seemed saturated with the scent of her, then it was gone, as if it had never been. Mitch headed for the back door as the thought finished with painful clarity; but he'd never be able to forget her.

HARLEY WAS ALONE most of the day. Mitch never came back, and the doctor called in once to say he was running late, so he wouldn't be home before going out to dinner. And Harley wasn't about to go after Mitch again. She couldn't bear to see the pain in the man, or to be so close she could feel it herself.

She couldn't forget what Mitch had said he'd do about Freeman, but she knew she couldn't follow through. When noon passed and Mitch still wasn't back, she went into Doc's office and put in a call to Ruth Dylan, her agent. The phone rang four times before the answering service picked it up, and when the woman asked for a message, she hesitated.

"This is Harley Madison. Just tell her that I'll call her again on Monday."

The woman dutifully repeated the message, then Harley hung up and sat back in the old swivel chair. The room wasn't large, but every bit of wall space was covered with photos, mostly black-and-white ones that had obviously been taken years ago.

She got up and scanned the pictures of the clinic when it had been an orphanage—some taken in the summer, with the trees in front blossoming with some pale flowers. In many, little children were lined up in a row under those trees, scrubbed and neat and very solemn.

She went from photo to photo, then stopped by one near the door—a black-and-white picture of a single little boy, maybe six or seven, with dark hair combed straight back from his serious face. The white shirt and stiff jeans looked new, but the look in the child's eyes was old. It was a look she'd seen before—of sadness. Not obvious sadness, but a deep one. And she knew the eyes were hazel.

She looked under it and saw in tiny printing, Mitchell Paul Rollins.

She touched the glass over the photo and was taken aback to note that she was trembling. It was painful to see Mitch, even as a child, all alone. The way he'd been most of his life, except for Doc. Why had she thought she had to be near Mitch to feel the shadow of his pain?

She drew back and left the room. As she started down the hall, she heard a phone ringing and stopped, ready to go back into Doc's office. But the sound was coming from past her room, from behind the closed door of the lab.

She hesitated, but when the phone kept ringing, she went in. In Mitch's bedroom she averted her eyes from the bed, which was still mussed from last night, and went to the desk under the windows.

She picked up the receiver. "Yes?"

There was silence, then a man's voice came over the line. "I'm sorry. I was trying to get in touch with someone, but I guess I have the wrong number."

"Who were you calling?"

"Mitch Rollins."

"This is his number."

"Who's this?"

"I'm staying at the clinic for a few days. Mitch isn't here right now, but I can take a message."

"I guess... Just tell him he needs to call Luke as soon as possible."

Luke Stewart. She fought her first instinct—to tell Luke what was happening. She bit her lip to keep the words inside. "I'll tell him."

"And tell him it's important that he calls me as soon as possible."

"I will," she said.

There was a click, then the line buzzed in her ear. Slowly she replaced the receiver, wishing she'd said something but knowing she didn't have a choice. She turned to leave, but stopped when she saw Mitch at the door. His expression was unreadable, that barrier once again firmly in place.

Mitch took off his jacket and hung it on a peg by the door. All day he'd had the feeling that Harley was haunting him. Even trudging miles through the snow didn't stop that. When he'd found the Jeep and dug into it through two feet of snow, the haunting had continued.

He'd found a note she'd left when she'd thought she was going to die. She was apologizing. God, he wanted to hold her and tell her that her living or dying wasn't something to apologize for. And to tell her that the thought of the world without her was almost unbearable for him.

Now she was here, in his room, looking so lovely that he found it difficult to even take a breath. He could run for hours without getting out of breath, but he couldn't look at her like this without gasping.

"Aren't things messed up enough without you being in here?" he asked as he raked his fingers through his hair. "Following me around won't change things...or change my mind."

She crossed her arms on her breasts, and he hated to see her acting defensive, but he knew that was better than her getting closer to him. "I didn't come in here to seduce you, if that's what you're thinking."

He almost smiled at the color that stained her cheeks. "Oh, is that so?"

"I heard the phone ringing and I thought—"

"The phone?"

"Yes, and it was your friend, Luke."

Luke called him once a week at scheduled times, not like this, and Harley had spoken to him. "What did he say?"

"He wants you to call him back as soon as you can. He said it's important."

Mitch knew it had to be important for Luke to call. Trying to block out Harley's presence, he dialed Luke's number and was frustrated when he got the answering machine. "It's me. I'm here," he said after the beep. "Call back."

He turned to Harley and asked, "How long ago did he call?"

"Just a minute ago."

Then a thought came to him. "What did you tell him?"

"Nothing. I wanted to, but I didn't."

"Thank you," he said softly, and meant it.

"Just let me say one thing, then I'll go."

"Could I stop you?"

"No."

"Go ahead."

"I know that you think you have to do this alone, but you have friends who would help you at the drop of a hat, and I would…" She bit her lip, then said softly, "I'd do anything to help you."

He felt his heart lurch. "Why? You hardly know me. I hardly know you."

She blinked rapidly, and he could see the brightness of tears in her eyes. He didn't want her to cry. He didn't think he could take that and stay where he was. "Do you have to ask me that?" she whispered.

He knew he should get the hell out of here, that he shouldn't say another thing, but he couldn't stop himself. "I shouldn't ask, should I?"

She looked at him with the bluest eyes he'd ever seen and uttered words that broke his heart. "I care about you, and I need you."

Harley said the words, then waited for the world to end. She waited for Mitch to tell her to get out, for him to scream at her, to tell her that he didn't care and didn't need her. Or worse, for him to laugh. But he didn't do any of that.

He stayed very still, but his voice was enough to run riot over her frayed nerves. "I don't want anyone to care or to need me," he said hoarsely.

Then her tears fell, and she knew exactly what they were for this time. For a child with no one. For a man with no one. And for herself, because she wanted this man so desperately and without him she had no one.

"I don't want to need you…or to care, but I do. Mitch, tell me how to stop caring, how to stop needing you." Her tears fell freely now, hot and silent, and she reached out to him, feeling his heart pound under her palms. "Please, tell me what to do," she sobbed.

He bowed his head and breathed, "I don't know. I don't know what to do."

"Let me stay."

"How can you?" He held his hands in front of him. "I can't even touch you."

Harley gently laid her hands in his. "But I can touch you." She stroked his jawline and smiled unsteadily at him. "Will you let me?"

She stood there waiting, feeling as if it took an eternity before Mitch said, "I don't know what could happen. If I lose control…"

She touched a finger to his lips. "I trust you, Mitch, I trust you."

"But I don't trust myself," he said, his breath hot against her hand.

"Then trust me," she breathed.

Mitch reached behind him and swung the door shut. "You have to promise me one thing," he said.

She was very still. "Anything."

"If you think there's any reason to be afraid of— of what could happen, you'll stop."

She laid her hands on his chest, her palms pressed against his strength. "I promise," she whispered, and lowered her hands to his belt. She tugged his T-shirt free of his jeans, then worked her fingers under the cotton. When she touched the silky heat of his stomach, she heard his sharp breath.

"Take your shirt off," she murmured, wanting to feel him, to see him, to know him.

When he did as she said, she saw his naked chest, the suggestion of dark hair that arrowed down his abdomen to the waist of his jeans. She touched her tongue to her lips and reached for his hand and caught it with hers. Lacing her fingers with his, she pulled his hand to her breast. "I'm not sure exactly how to do this," she admitted, wishing she could smile and make a joke out of it. But her heart was too deeply involved to laugh.

He pulled back from her, taking his hand from hers, then went past her. When she turned, he was by the bed, his hand on the button of his jeans. "Let's start at the beginning."

She went to him, getting to her knees on the bed to bring herself to his eye level. She cupped his face between her hands, rubbing his cheeks with her thumbs, and she found a smile that she didn't know was there. "That sounds like a plan to me," she whispered, then kissed him.

His taste coursed through her, his heat invaded her as his breath mingled with hers, and she slipped her arms around his neck. She pulled him closer to her, holding on to him, wanting to be closer than was humanly possible. If she could have melted into him, she would have, to be surrounded by him, to have every pore in her being covered by him. She wanted him in her soul, wanted him to be a part of her forever.

She wanted his arms around her, to feel him pull her to him, his hands demanding more and more from her. But he didn't touch her. The only contact was where she touched him, where their lips met. Awkwardly, she tried to change places with him, to get him back on the bed, but she tumbled backward. For an instant, she felt his body over hers, his hard strength against her softness, then it was gone.

He braced himself with his hands on either side of her, his arms tensely supporting his weight, suspending him above her. His legs were between hers, his thighs pressed against her, and for a moment, she let herself imagine what it would be like. With her eyes closed she could see him over her, his hips against hers, then his strength testing her and filling her.

She arched to him and she heard him groan, a deep, raw sound that startled her. Her eyes flew open and she was faced with what it was costing him to not move. His face was distorted, his lips almost bloodless, and his hair fell forward, shadowing his eyes. She could feel the tension in him, the fight he was putting up to keep some semblance of control.

Her heart ached for him, and for herself, and it was bittersweet being there. She touched his face gently, then slipped away from him. "Just lie down," she said softly. "It's okay."

He moved back, and for a moment she felt a wrenching fear that he was going to stop. But the next thing she knew he was undoing his jeans. Without embarrassment, he stepped out of the denim, then took off his undershorts, which barely contained his desire. Then he was there in front of her, with nothing to hide the effect she was having on him.

She couldn't move. She took in every detail, letting it sear into her mind, then he was coming toward her, getting onto the bed by her, and as she moved to one side, he lay down by her.

He got onto his side, supporting himself on one elbow, his eyes burning into hers. Then he lifted his other hand to touch her, but drew back with an oath that was shattering in its intensity, his hand curled into a fist.

Harley went to him. She got on her knees, and

never looking away from Mitch, stripped off her blouse and her bra.

The lacy cups fell away, and just the potency of his eyes on her tightened her nipples. It was as if he'd touched her, as if he'd kissed her, and they were hard buds, swelling under his gaze.

"My God," he groaned, "you're beautiful…beautiful. And I want you."

By his words she was driven to unsnap her pants and tug them off. Her panties were all the barrier left, and they were gone in one movement, then she was before him.

"Come here," he said. And she did.

Stretching alongside him, she reached out and found his strength. The contact brought a shuddering moan from Mitch, deep and jarring, and his hips arched toward her touch. She stroked him as she partially rolled onto him, close enough to taste his lips, then his jaw, then the pulse that beat at the hollow of his throat.

Mitch felt her mouth move lower on him as she stoked him with a fiery demand that drew at the core of his being. The sensations were overwhelming, and he was losing himself in a vortex of need that threatened to consume him. When her mouth found his nipple, when her hand moved faster on him, he jerked back, a fear so raw and deep in him that it had no name hurling him into a place he wasn't sure he'd ever come back from.

"Stop," he gasped. "Stop."

He felt her freeze, then her hands and mouth leave him. But he didn't want that. He didn't want her to stop. Slowly he opened his eyes, and she was right there, her face mere inches from his.

"Mitch, I...is it all right?" she asked in a tremulous whisper. "Do you want me to stop?"

"God, no," he breathed. "I want you."

In one quick motion she was over him, straddling his hips, and he could feel her against him. He arched back and entered her, filling her as if they'd been made for each other.

His hands ached from their hold on the bed linen, and he fought the need to thrust deeper into her. As if she knew, Harley lowered herself onto him, and he heard her moan softly. When he looked up, her eyes were closed, her head thrown back and her hands braced on his chest. Then, with aching slowness, she moved, and his world was filled with an ecstasy that was almost unbearable.

Mitch felt the universe center on that moment, and as she moved on him, he knew an exquisite agony that blurred the line between pain and pleasure. It grew and grew, and as her fingers dug into his flesh, as her heat consumed him, he knew that if this was all he was to have in life, his life would be worthwhile. It was all for this moment, for this second, for this heartbeat.

When he heard Harley cry out, he knew he

couldn't bear it any longer. He couldn't stop himself from thrusting and joining in. His voice mingled with hers, and he felt the explosion that sent him into a place where everything was right, everything was perfect and everything was possible.

HARLEY CAME OUT of a place of shattering pleasure and slowly leaned down until she was resting against Mitch's chest. She'd been looking for this all of her life; she knew that with a simplicity that was astounding to her. This place. This man. A lifelong search was over, and she felt a peace she'd never known.

She tasted his skin, the salty dampness pungent on her lips, and she whispered, "Thank you," knowing that the words didn't even come close to what she owed him for this. She had only a shadow of an idea what it cost him to let her be with him, and she loved him for that.

Her mouth stilled on him as that thought sank in, settling in her heart. God, she loved him. She must have loved him all the time. And it seemed so right, so natural. She rested her face in the hollow of his throat, then slowly broke the connection between them and rolled onto her side, his arm under her neck.

She snuggled against him, laying her leg over his thighs, and she heard his heart beating in her ear. When she spread her hand on his stomach, he shifted slightly, able to get a bit closer without putting his arm around her. She ached for his embrace. But this would have to be enough, and it would be, for as long as it lasted.

"I told you we could make it happen," she said with a sigh.

"You made it happen." His voice rumbled against her ear.

She closed her eyes for a moment, absorbing the peace that surrounded her like a warm blanket, then rose on her elbow and looked down at Mitch. The late-afternoon sun filtered into the room, cool and clean, exposing the planes and angles of his face. The line of his jaw, the way his mouth turned up ever so slightly at the corners, the fine lines at his eyes. With a decidedly unsteady hand, she smoothed his hair back from his damp forehead.

"I wish we could stay here like this forever," she breathed.

Mitch narrowed his eyes on her, then very carefully touched her cheek with just the tips of his fingers. "Nothing lasts forever," he said, his voice husky with a desire that she could feel echoing in her.

She lowered her head and kissed him, almost tentatively at first. Then, as his lips opened, any restraint on her part was gone. The kiss was deep and searching, a taste of the man who had seeped into her soul. Even though she'd felt sated moments ago, desire inflamed her again. She wanted to touch him, to explore him, to know him once more. Her hand skimmed over his chest, to his stomach, then lower, and she knew that the desire wasn't one-sided at all.

Feeling the effect she had on him fanned the fire of the intense need for him to fill her, till she could barely breathe. She moved over him and he entered her with an ease that should have come from years of being lovers. There was no gradual building up of feelings, but an immediate explosion of white-hot flame that all but consumed her.

In that single moment she felt as if she were one with Mitch, joined forever in a bond that could never be broken. Arching back, she let herself go, into the sensations that surrounded her and possessed her.

From a great distance she heard Mitch cry out, then she fell forward onto him and whispered, "Forever," into the heat of his tangled hair and sleek skin.

The last thing she heard before drifting into a deep, wonderful sleep was Mitch echoing, "Forever."

Chapter Twelve

Mitch lay with a sleeping Harley until the light started to fade and he could see the colors of the setting sun splash the winter sky. He burned everywhere she touched him and tried not to move. He'd never thought this would be possible, yet it was more than he'd ever dreamed of. Memories of their time together flashed before him, stirring him again, and when he felt his body begin to tighten, he turned to look at her.

In the dimness, with her dark hair tangled around her face, she was breathtaking. He studied everything about her, letting it sear into his mind, wanting to take her into him and keep her there forever. But when he lifted his hand to touch her, he could see it was shaking. Gingerly he made the contact, touching just the tip of his forefinger to the pulse that beat at the hollow of her throat.

Her heartbeat echoed his, and a bonding that had begun that first moment he met her intensified. For a moment he allowed himself to think about the future, about a time when the formula was out of his system, when he could hold her and touch her and explore her freely. But his dream was cut short when the phone rang.

Harley stirred and he whispered, "Shh, I'll get that." He padded across the cool floor naked, to grab the phone before it could ring a third time.

He put the receiver to his ear, but never took his eyes off the woman in his bed as he whispered, "Yes?"

"Oh, God, Mitch, finally," Luke practically shouted over the line. "Man, why didn't you call me back? Didn't that woman give you the message?"

"She did and I did. I left a message on your machine."

"Oh, I got so involved that I forgot to tell the woman I wasn't at home."

"It's a holiday, Luke, so I assumed—"

"I'm at the lab."

Mitch turned his back to Harley and said in a low voice, "Why?"

"I came down here yesterday to run control checks on the subjects and ended up running a few tissue samples on four of them."

"I thought you were monitoring, but not doing anything else until I could figure this out?"

"I was, until I got down here and saw the change in them."

"What change?"

"They were obviously stronger. They have no sleep cycle, and their food cycle was erratic. I decided to take four of them, get tissue samples and take blood, then I could run the tests while the lab's closed for the holiday."

Mitch heard Harley stir behind him, and he glanced over his shoulder at her. She was awake, lying on her side, the sheet around her waist and her breasts exposed, inviting, tantalizing. But it was the soft smile on her face that made his heart lurch.

"Just get to the bottom line."

"I ran the samples, and not more than five minutes later, they each went into a seizure of some sort. Their temps dropped quickly, and they had tremors, forcing them into the fetal position."

Mitch closed his eyes tightly as the words coming over the line sank in. "And?"

"It's amazing. The patches on their stomachs where I took the samples were—"

It was the serum. Spontaneous healing. "They were healing, weren't they?"

"You don't sound shocked by this."

"Just tell me. Am I right?"

"Yes, but there's more." He could hear Luke take a deep breath before finishing. "Mitch, they died. All of them died within half an hour of the testing.''

A rush of excitement was ripped away from him, suddenly and completely. ''What?''

''They're dead. I'll run postmortems on them in a bit, but I had to let you know so you can monitor yourself. I'm worried. You need to come back here so I can monitor you.''

''No,'' he said. ''I won't.''

''Then promise me you'll call me if anything happens, and I'll get there on a charter as soon as I can.''

''Sure,'' Mitch said flatly.

''You're having symptoms, aren't you? Mitch, why didn't you tell me? I'll be there—''

''No, I have to think. Stay where you are and I'll call you back later. Just wait for my call.'' He closed his eyes so tightly colors exploded behind his lids. All he could think of was Harley, and what would happen now. Why had he thought there could be a future? It was all a stupid fantasy. It wasn't spontaneous healing, it was spontaneous death. He took a breath and spoke quickly in a low voice. ''Just do your work on that end and I'll call you back. Later.''

Luke hung up and Mitch tried to draw a breath into his tight lungs while his friend's words echoed in his mind. *Mitch, they died. All of them, they died...*

"Mitch?"

He heard Harley say his name and he looked up, bracing himself. Yet nothing prepared him for the sight of her in the partial light, naked, beautiful and coming toward him. Her hair tumbled around her bare shoulders, and if he'd ever seen anything more wonderful in his life, he couldn't remember. Or anything more painful to behold.

He knew in that moment that he had no dreams left. And Harley wasn't part of his future. He had no future. But she was the best thing in his past, the best thing in his life. And that life was almost over. Memories of the way she'd touched him came to him, and he knew that he never wanted pity or sympathy from her, not after he'd had her love. He was in this alone, and that was the way it was going to be until it was over.

"That was your friend Luke, wasn't it?" she asked.

"Yeah, he needed to tell me something." Mitch wasn't at all sure how to go about doing what he knew he had to do. "Some information I needed."

"What information?"

"It's not important." With Harley so close to him he felt his body stir, and when he thought about what he was about to do to her, he felt vaguely ill. He'd lost control over his life, ever since he'd injected himself with that godawful serum.

When his eyes followed Harley's down to his

hand clutching the phone receiver, he realized just how little control he really had. The receiver was crushed.

"Dammit!" When Harley reached for the broken receiver, Mitch yanked it back and dropped it on the phone with a loud clatter.

"Mitch, what did Luke say?"

"It doesn't matter. You need to get out of here." He turned from her and grabbed his jeans and T-shirt and put them on. Without looking at her he pulled another shirt out of the drawer and tossed it to her across the room. "Here, put this on."

She did what he said without arguing, and when she looked at him with those blue eyes, with his T-shirt caressing her thighs and her breasts swelling under the cotton, he knew that he loved her. It came to him in a single moment, a fact so simple, so painfully clear, that he didn't even fight it. He loved her. He'd loved her before he knew who she was, before she'd touched him, before she'd smiled at him or kissed him. He loved her with a passion that defied logic. And he'd never have it again. He'd never have her again.

"Mitch, tell me what's going on," she said as she came closer to him.

"You have to go," he said harshly. "You have to get out of here and get back to your life in L.A., and forget that you ever met me."

She dissolved the rest of the buffer space between them, and he could hardly bear to look at her. "How can I do that?" she asked softly, her ebony hair falling in a riot around the stark whiteness of the T-shirt.

"You have to."

"How can I after all this? I don't understand. It worked, Mitch, I'm fine, and it was good. You saw that we can be together." High color touched her delicate cheeks. "It worked."

He braced himself, then said words that hurt him as much as he knew they were going to hurt her. But she'd heal from the words. She would never heal from what he was or what he could do to her. Or from watching him when the end came. "Sure it worked. It was fun. Is that what you want to hear? We had a good time, but it's over. It's that simple."

"A good time?" she breathed.

He hated the pain he could see etching her mouth and eyes. And he hated himself for putting it there. But he could bear that if it saved her. He pushed on, driving a wedge between them that he prayed would make her turn and walk out of this room, out of this place and out of this nightmare.

After she was gone, he'd have to learn to deal with his grief over what might have been.

"Lady, have you looked in the mirror lately? God, you're beautiful. You've made your fortune being every man's dream. The American Dream. Why would I be any different?"

The raw pain that flashed in her eyes was almost his undoing, but he made himself stand there and watch.

"How…?" She gasped, then pressed a hand to her middle. "That's a lie. You—you can't mean that."

"But I do. Just leave, and we can both get on with our lives."

She stood in front of him, her eyes wide, her chin trembling. "Is that what you really want?"

He'd told lies in his time, but this one almost choked him—a single word that seared him to the soul. "Yes."

Harley barely covered a gasp at the pain that racked her at his words. For whatever reason, she'd believed in the fantasy that he would love her and want her forever. Now it was smashed by one word. It had all been a lie, and she'd bought into it because she'd wanted to so desperately.

He narrowed his eyes on her, an expression that she knew by now meant he was shutting himself off even more. "When Doc gets back, he can take you to Dumbarton and you're out of here."

"Just like that?"

"Just like that," he echoed, and almost felt a physical barrier growing between them.

She faced the naked truth—that she loved him and he didn't love her. It was her looks, "the package," as Freeman called it. She cringed when she remembered the way she'd almost begged him to let her make love with him. Thankfully, before she could fall apart, a certain anger came to her rescue. "You got what you wanted, and that's it. So long, and don't slam the door on my way out," she muttered.

He raked his hands roughly through his hair. "I never said that. But the fact is, this is it. There isn't any more."

Harley had never felt so alone, or felt such an anger in her. "Should I say thank you?"

"Just say goodbye and go back to your multi-million-dollar contract. You'll get past that garbage in your past, and you'll have it all."

She'd have it all? What a total lie that statement was. "I don't want—"

"No, don't even say it." He shook his head. "That's exactly what you want, and you want it so badly that you left Texas and went west and fought through a ton of odds to get where you are. You want it, lady, and you'll get it. This is just a bump in the road for you. Nothing more." He took a rough breath, then said, "Now get out of here. I left your things in your room. In the morning you'll walk away from here and never look back."

She wished she could say that she hated him— him and his words, which were cutting through her. She wished she could say she didn't care, that she wasn't going to look back. But all she could manage was, "Sure."

"And all of this—the lab, the serum—has to be kept quiet. You understand that, don't you?"

"Oh, I understand that. Your secret is safe with me. You even sealed the bargain, didn't you?" she muttered, then turned from Mitch. Blindly she grabbed her rumpled clothes off the foot of the bed. She didn't look back as she headed for the door. "I'm out of here now. I don't have to wait until morning."

"What does that mean?" he called after her.

She stopped in the doorway, but kept her eyes on the lab in front of her. "Dumbarton's close by. I can walk into town and find someplace to stay until morning."

"That's stupid. Wait for Doc and he'll take you."

She wasn't going to argue with him. She was just going to get out of here as soon as she could. There was still some light outside and she could make it before dark.

"Lady, are you—"

She cut him off with "My name is Harley, not Lady," then walked away and didn't stop until she was in her room. Her purse and duffel bag from the wreck were lying just inside the door. She dropped her rumpled clothes, then quickly stripped off Mitch's T-shirt and changed into fresh jeans and a sweater. She put on her jacket and grabbed her purse and duffel bag. A glance out the windows told her the light was failing rapidly. If she hurried, she could get to town before it got too dark. She stepped out of her room into silence. Mitch wasn't anywhere in sight.

As she approached Doc's office, she hesitated, then went inside. Putting her things down, she snapped on the desk light and grabbed the phone.

She dialed Ruth's number again, and this time the woman answered. "Ruth, it's me, Harley."

"Hey, Harley, I got your message, but I'm glad you called. Good news, I think. The Tara Gaye reps have pretty much agreed to all our terms. We've got it made. You're going to be the new American Dream."

"That's nice."

"Hey, you sounded happier when I told you I was going to the store. Are you all right?"

Harley closed her eyes. "Ruth, I need to talk to you. I'll come by your office first thing Monday morning and explain some things to you."

"What's going on?"

"Too much to tell you over the phone. Just be there at nine and I'll meet you."

"No hints?"

"I'll tell you everything then."

"It's not anything to do with Tara Gaye, is it? You haven't changed your mind, have you?"

"No, I haven't."

"Then you'd better tell me, and tell me now. I'm not a patient person when so much money's on the line."

"Okay," Harley said, and sat on the edge of the desk. Quickly she told her about Freeman and the arrest, then said, "And I'm not going to let him do it to me."

"Good God, what are you going to do?"

"I'm going public. I want to get an interview with a reputable magazine and tell my side of the story. Then he can take a flying leap."

"So can your career," Ruth said, her tone unreadable.

"Yes, it could, but I don't think it will. I think people will understand, and it can be a cautionary tale for others. And Ruth, if you can't back me on this, I'll understand."

Ruth was silent for a moment, then said, "You're right. The spin is everything. We'll cut this guy off at the pass."

"You'll help me?"

"Damn straight I will. And I think it's a gutsy move on your part. Let me do the dirty work, and you just take care of the face and body."

"Yeah, the face and body," Harley muttered.

"Get back here by nine on Monday and I'll have everything set up for you. Okay?"

"I'll be there."

"Good girl," Ruth said, then hung up.

Harley felt one load drop off her shoulders, but the other burden was the one she wasn't sure she could carry. She reached for her purse, got her wallet and took out all of the money she had with her, except for enough to get some food. She laid the bills on the desk, anchored them with a pen holder, then picked up her purse.

She took one last look at the picture on the wall of the somber little boy. The eyes haunted her the way the man's words did. Her face and body. That was all she'd been for so long that she'd forgotten there was a real person inside, a person who could love and hurt. And right now, that pain was raw and deep. A face and a body. She bit her lip hard and left the office.

When she opened the front door she was met by the deep cold of the early evening. She glanced to the right and could make out a glow beyond the trees. The town. She could reach it. Hunching into the growing wind, she went down the snow-banked steps to the driveway, which was almost completely obliterated by the storms. Only two vague indentations showed where the doctor's car had left early that morning.

Snow crunched under her boots and she sank almost to her knees but she slowly made her way toward the double gates that stood open to the road. The landscape looked like something out of a fairy tale. The last rays of the cool light glinted off the icy boughs of the ancient fir trees, and huge snow-flakes fell from the leaden sky.

But this was no fairy tale with a happily-ever-after ending. Not even close.

She struggled through the snow, and as she got to the gates, she wondered if it was stupid of her to let Mitch force her out of the house. But when she heard her name coming to her on the wind that was swirling the snowflakes, she knew she wasn't stupid at all. Mitch was calling her. And she knew that by leaving, she was surviving.

"Harley?" She heard it again, and finally turned at the gates. Mitch was in the open door of the clinic. A man alone, just the way he wanted it, his features hidden by the shadows of the coming evening. She turned and hurried as quickly as she could through the gates.

She rounded the snow-shrouded gatepost to the right, and a huge black truck was there before she knew what was happening. She never heard it coming, and now it was driving right at her. Before she could move to get out of the way, it swerved to the right, hit a snowbank on the other side of the road and went nose down off the road into the piled snow.

It was over so quickly, Harley barely had time to comprehend what had happened. But there was the truck, silent in the snowbank, its back end sticking up awkwardly.

"Oh, my God," Harley gasped. She tried to get to the driver but the snow held her back, making her feel as if she was running in place.

Before she could move, Mitch was past her in a blur of motion. He was dressed only in the T-shirt and jeans.

"Doc? Doc?" he called, cutting easily through the snow to get to the driver's door. "Hey, Doc?"

The whole front of the truck's hood was buried in the drift, and from the way it angled down, it must have found a ditch hidden by the snow. Harley could hear Doc call out, "Mitch, it's okay. I'm all right. But the door's jammed."

Mitch glanced at Harley, then reached for the handle, and she could see the veins in his arms bulge as he pulled evenly on the door. There was a groaning sound, then a crack and the door was open. Doc was there, staring at Mitch as if he'd seen a ghost, then, shaking himself, stepped out of the truck. He sank into snow up to his thighs as he turned to Harley.

"My God, girl, I could have killed you. I didn't see you there until I was turning in. Right scared me to death."

"It scared me, too," she admitted, her heart still hammering in her chest.

"And what are you doing out here, anyway?" he asked, eyeing the duffel bag in her hands.

"I was walking into town."

"What? In this weather, at this time of the day? You haven't got more than ten minutes of light left, and the road is almost impassable. You California people, you just don't have a clue about this country, do you?"

"I guess not," she said, her face starting to tingle with the cold.

The doctor turned to Mitch. "And you, out here in your shirtsleeves—you'll catch your death of cold. Get back inside. I've got enough business without you being a patient here." He reached into the truck and took out his doctor's bag. "Let's get inside."

Mitch motioned them to go ahead. "Take Harley back inside with you, warm up, and I'll see if I can get this truck out of here."

"Don't even try," Doc said. "She's buried."

"Just go inside."

"Stubborn cuss," Doc muttered, but he didn't argue anymore. He looked at Harley. "Well, you and I will do the sensible thing and get inside." Then he glanced at Mitch. "There's an extra jacket in there. At least put it on."

"Sure," Mitch said, then climbed into the cab and closed the door with a snap.

The doctor came to Harley and took her arm,

then urged her toward the gates. "I don't know about you, but I need a good cup of hot chocolate. How does that sound?"

She looked at Mitch in the cab, just a shadow of him visible, then turned and went with the older man. At least she wouldn't be alone in there with Mitch for the night. "Yes, something warm sounds good."

They walked back to the clinic, but as they neared the front door, Harley heard something. Turning at the same time as Doc, she saw the truck coming through the gates, crushing a pathway through the snow.

"Well, I'll be...." the doctor muttered as he watched the truck coming toward them. "He got it out of there. I called him stubborn, but I should have known Mitch could do it, if anyone could. It's a miracle."

"Yes, a miracle," Harley breathed as the truck got closer. Mitch had done it himself, and she didn't have to ask how. He was the miracle.

They got to the bottom of the steps just as the truck came to a stop nearby and the door squeaked open. Harley saw Mitch's face and knew something was very wrong. He was pale and sleek with sweat, then his eyes met hers with a look she'd seen before. He gripped the door frame and got out, and that was when she saw his jeans torn across the thighs. And the blood. Everywhere.

Chapter Thirteen

"Mitch," she gasped, rushing to him. "What happened?"

"The frame...the weight of the frame...I didn't realize it until..." His tongue touched his lips. "I have to get inside."

Doc was there by Harley, and without saying a word, he looped Mitch's arm around his shoulder and took the brunt of his weight. "We have to get him into the ER. Damn it, boy, you should have left it in the ditch. No one had be anywhere tonight."

Mitch closed his eyes and muttered through clenched teeth, "Take—take me to my room."

"We'll get you in the examination—"

"No," Mitch gasped. "My room."

"Wherever," Doc said. "Just hold on to me."

"And me," Harley said, as she slipped her arm around Mitch's waist to try and take some of the load off of Doc.

Mitch felt so cold, far beyond what should have been from the outside air. That horrible cold. It was just like the first time. Then, as they neared the door, he started to shake, and she knew it was happening all over again.

By the time they got Mitch into his room, he was shaking so hard his teeth were chattering. He felt icy cold and his skin was damp. Harley helped ease him back into the same bed where they'd made love, but that seemed an eternity ago now.

As he collapsed onto the rumpled sheets, Doc snapped, "Get his shoes off, while I find some scissors to cut his jeans off so we can get a look at the damage."

It was easier for Harley to do exactly what she was told than to think right then. By the time she had tugged off his boots, Doc was back with the scissors. He sliced the denim and ripped the material clear of Mitch's legs. As the jeans fell aside, Harley could barely look at his wounds.

They cut deep, straight across the middle of his thighs, but despite all the blood on his pants, they were hardly bleeding now. As Doc bent over Mitch to examine him, he said, "Hold his feet still if you can so I can get a good look."

Harley looked at Mitch. His eyes were closed and the veins in his neck and shoulders were very visible under his skin, which was sheened with sweat. His jaw was clenched and she could tell he was fighting whatever was happening with every atom of his being. Her heart ached. She needed to do something, but all she could do was hold him.

"Tell me what's going on," Doc said to Mitch.

Mitch never opened his eyes. "Body temp's dropping. Involuntary muscle spasms."

"And the wounds, Mitch, the wounds?"

"What?" he gasped as another round of shivering started.

"They're healing right in front of my eyes." Doc cast a sharp look at Harley. "Do you know what's happening?"

Mitch couldn't answer, the chills were wracking his body so badly, and Harley said quickly, "He's been doing experiments on himself and this happened before when he cut his hand. That's why the gash looked so small when you saw it. It's shock, isn't it?"

"No, it's not. I don't know what it is, but I'm calling for the lifeline flight right now. We can have you in Dumbarton in half an hour if the weather cooperates."

"No," Mitch gasped as he rolled onto his left side and curled his legs up to his middle. "No hospital...no one...just Luke."

"Luke?"

"Luke Stewart," Harley said, moving to the side of the bed to take hold of Mitch's clenched hand. "He's been working on this with Mitch. He'll know what to do." She held on to him and leaned close. "Mitch, what's Luke's phone number?"

"On...desk," he managed to communicate in a hoarse, strangled voice. "Home...lab...."

Harley looked at Doc, but the older man was staring at Mitch's legs. The wounds were still visible, but the flesh was continuing to mend, right in front of their eyes. "Mitch, I don't know what's going on, but you need a hospital. I can't do anything for you here."

"Call Luke," Mitch whispered hoarsely. "Call."

Doc hesitated, then crossed the room. "Watch him," he said to Harley. "Keep him as still as you can, and I'll..." He stopped by the phone, touched the crushed receiver, then without saying a thing about it, picked up a small address book and headed for the door. "I'll call from my office. I'll be back as soon as I can. Meanwhile, get those blankets over him."

Harley nodded, but never took her eyes off Mitch. She could almost see the path of his pain, flushing his skin, racking his body. The coldness was as devastating as the shaking. "Hold on, Mitch, hold on. Doc's going to call Luke and he'll help. Please, just hold on."

"I didn't..." He touched his tongue to his lips as the shaking eased a bit, and he whispered hoarsely, "Never wanted...you seeing this."

At first she didn't realize what he'd said, then

she understood. "You knew, didn't you? That's why Luke called. To tell you about this?"

He nodded, a jerky motion with his head. "Lab subjects...same thing..."

She touched his cold, damp face. "You tried to make me leave, didn't you?"

He was very still for a moment, his eyes open and glazed with deep pain and intense sadness. "I had to. I—I knew...Luke told me...I knew—"

"Damn you, you could have told me! You could have trusted me."

"I...couldn't trust...myself." He took a sharp breath, then exhaled on a hiss. She could feel his body tensing again.

"Mitch, what did Luke do for them, for the lab subjects?" He was starting to shake again and his eyes closed tightly. "Mitch, Mitch, just listen to me. Please. Tell me what Doc can do."

He uttered a single word. "Nothing."

"No, there has to be something. Tell me! Anything—he'll do it. We'll try. Dammit, Mitch, we can't just do nothing!"

He swallowed convulsively, and his jaw clenched as he muttered through his teeth. "They died."

Harley couldn't absorb the words. She wouldn't. "Mitch, no. There has to be something, some way to stop this. I'll do anything. Just tell me, tell me."

"Nothing," he said in such a low voice that she could barely make it out now.

His color was ashen, his skin filmed with moisture, and he was shaking harder. "Doc!" she screamed. "Doc, come here. Mitch, you can't die. I won't let you. Do you hear me? I won't let you."

She touched his cheek. "You can't leave me. I just found you. Mitch..." He wasn't responding to anything but his own pain now. "God, no, don't let this happen," she prayed as she scrambled onto the bed with him.

She reached for the blankets and tugged them up and over both of them. Then she pulled Mitch to her, trying to absorb the tremors, trying to warm him. "Oh, God, Mitch don't do this," she sobbed. "I love you."

Tears choked her as she moved back enough to look into his face. She flinched at the pain etching his features, and she had never loved him more. "Don't leave me, please. I'm not going to leave you. I'll never leave you."

Suddenly the tremors eased, his body lost some tension and his eyes fluttered open. For one wonderful moment he was looking at her, his vision clear, and he breathed, "Lady, you never give up, do you?"

She touched his cheek, a surge of hope springing to life in her, but the next instant it was gone. The shaking came back with a vengeance, clenching his whole body, and Harley pulled him to her. "I'll love you forever," she murmured, holding him as tightly as she could.

"For the rest of my life?" he managed to gasp.

"No, for the rest of *my* life," she said, and held onto him as if she could take all of his pain, all of his suffering, and banish it.

Mitch was lost in a haze of cold and pain, but a part of him knew a peace that was startling. She loved him. And he would have given everything he'd ever had for one more hour with her. One more moment where he could hold her.

Her arms surrounded him, her essence filled him, and in some ironic spin of fate, he knew that this was the worst and the best moment of his life. Then he realized that he couldn't feel her heat anymore. He couldn't hear her heart, and he felt panicked for a moment, then it was gone.

He had a sense of floating toward a grayness, and he fought it. He raged against it, struggling to get free of it, to stay with Harley, to let her anchor him. But no matter how he struggled, the sensations got stronger and his sense of Harley got fainter.

"Mitch," he heard Harley whisper from a great distance. "Just hold on. Luke'll know something so Doc will be able to help you."

Without warning the shaking stopped, and the grayness was there, nudging at his feet, then his legs, and the pain was gone. He opened his eyes, and Harley was just inches from him in the tangle of sheets and pillows. So close, so dear. The love of his life.

"Oh, lady," he whispered, and managed to lift his hand and touch her cheek. He knew he was touching her, that his palm rested on her skin, but he couldn't really feel her. And he cursed the grayness that was robbing him of everything but the vision of her face.

It was over. And his heart ached for what could have been. For what he'd denied himself by one stupid act. Her hand covered his on her face, but there was no connection anymore. He knew he was still close to her, but he could feel a distance growing between them. He had to struggle to finally be able to say, "Lady, I...love you."

Then the grayness took him.

Harley heard Mitch's words, then saw his eyes flutter shut. His hand grew heavy on her cheek and would have slipped down to the sheets if she wasn't holding it. She held it to her face, whispering, "Mitch, no. Mitch! No, no, you'll be all right, I promise. I'm stubborn, you know that, and I'm not giving up. I promise you, I'll never give up."

She kissed his hair and held his hand as tightly as she could, her tears, oddly enough, deserting her. Her eyes were hot and gritty, and she brushed his hair back, kissing his temple, then his closed eyes. "Please, love, I can't do this. I can't. I—I love you. I love you."

But he didn't move. There were no more convulsions, no more shaking. In a frenzy of raging pain, she let go of his hand and pulled him to her. "No, no, no," she gasped, barely able to absorb the agony that ripped through her. She wouldn't let this happen. She couldn't. She rubbed his back, then kissed him again on his forehead, his eyes, his lips, fighting against the cold emptiness she was touching.

"You can't leave me," she sobbed. "You can't leave me. Oh, God, no, you can't. I can't live without you. I don't want to."

She caught his face between her hands. "Mitch, look at me. Mitch." She kissed his cold cheek, then his lips again. "Please, God, no," she sobbed.

She put her arms around him, pulling him to her, wishing she could just lose herself in him. "I love you," she wept softly. "I love you." She buried her face in his chest and felt her world dissolve into a blur of shattered dreams.

At first Harley didn't feel the hand on her shoulder, then Doc was easing her back. Doc was there, and she moved back enough for him to examine Mitch. Through her tears, she saw him press his fingers to Mitch's neck just under his ear. "Do something," she sobbed quietly. "Do something."

He methodically checked Mitch over. Then, as he moved back, Harley realized that his eyes were bright with tears. "He's gone," he whispered as he looked at her, his face pale and so sad. "My God, he's gone."

"No, you have to do something." She grabbed his arm, not letting him go. "Do whatever Luke said. He can't be dead. He can't."

"Harley, it's over."

She searched his eyes, but found only pain that echoed hers. "You can't just let him go."

Doc shook his head. "Child," he said in a low, unsteady voice, "I don't know what happened between you and Mitch, but it's over. Luke said there wasn't anything to do. I thought..." He took a shuddering breath. "There's nothing I or anyone can do. Luke told me this would happen. He just didn't know it would come so quickly. He's flying up, and he asked that we don't do anything until he gets here."

Harley slowly released her grip on Doc and sank back on her heels, then turned and looked down at Mitch. After all the pain and agony, she was shocked that he looked so peaceful. As if he was just sleeping. Just resting. She laid her hand over his heart and for a flickering moment in time, she thought she felt it beat. Then there was nothing.

"He had to come here," she whispered. "He came back, because this is all he ever had."

"I knew he was special from the first, that he was bright and eager to learn. I wanted him to become a doctor, to take over here when I couldn't do it any longer. He had the heart for it, but he got so sidetracked out there.'' Doc took a ragged breath. "He never told me. I asked him, and he never told me.''

Harley closed her eyes tightly and imagined that all she had to do was to open them and Mitch would be looking at her, his eyes narrowed with that squinty smile. And he'd say, "Lady, I love you."

But she didn't open her eyes. She couldn't. "I love you, Mitch," she whispered as she slowly rested her head on his chest, and tears finally came to her in a burning rush.

HARLEY STAYED with Mitch. She sat by him on the bed, holding his limp hand, just being there, unable to let go completely. The room grew dark, a wind started outside and snow began to fall heavily. But she stayed until a low light flashed on and she saw Doc come in, followed by a solid-looking blond-haired man.

The stranger was in a long overcoat, damp at his shoulders from the snow, and his short hair was mussed from the wind that rattled the windows.

"Luke Stewart," he said to Harley without her asking, then he looked past her at Mitch. He seemed to be bracing himself as he came closer, bringing the cool crispness of the night with him. His face was tight and unreadable, all except for the eyes. She could see sadness in them. And she was thankful for a certain numbness that had come to her rescue sometime in the darkness. It shrouded her, protected her. For now, it was in place.

"I wish he'd told me," he said softly. Then he shook his head. "I'll make arrangements for everything." He looked at Harley, then Doc. "I think you both understand what's happened, and that this can't go any farther than the three of us?"

"How are you going to explain his death?" Doc asked.

"I've told the people at the lab that he'd been unwell, that that's why he took the sabbatical, so I'll go with that story."

"Can you bury him here?" Doc said.

"Yes, that might be best. I can take care of things at the lab."

Harley felt as if she was going mad. They were talking so dispassionately, these two men who were the only friends Mitch had in this life. And they were making arrangements, worrying about what people would think. It felt like madness to Harley, worrying about what people thought. She felt sick when she considered all the time she'd wasted worrying about the world when she'd had Mitch alive, right there.

Luke looked at Harley again, and before she could say anything, he murmured, "We haven't met, but we talked on the phone. I presume that was you?"

She nodded.

Then she saw that look, a slight widening of his eyes, that sense that he'd just remembered something. And she wasn't wrong. "That suntan lotion, the one with the funny-looking bottle. You—you were in that commercial, weren't you?"

"Yes," she managed to answer, her voice flat in her own ears.

"I don't know why you're here, but Mitch must have trusted you with this. And you know that there can't be any press on this. None."

"I gave him my word," she said. "No one will know."

"Thank you," Luke murmured. "We can make arrangements and have a private burial before I go back."

Burial. The word was stark and ugly, and Harley could feel it nudging at the numbness around her. She fought it back, then turned to Mitch and took his hand in hers. She needed that contact one last time. "He has no one but us," she breathed.

"He wanted it that way," Luke said.

She shook her head. "He was so alone. His whole life, he was so alone."

Luke was silent for a long moment, then Harley felt him come closer and gently touch her shoulder. The warmth in his fingers was a horrible contrast to Mitch's cold hand in hers, and she knew it was time to go.

She gently put his hand down on the sheet, then touched his chest over his heart. "I love you," she breathed, then slowly drew back and got off the bed.

She didn't look around as she walked on shaky legs to the door and out into the lab. As she went through the room and up the stairs into the silent hall, she pulled that numbness tightly around her. She knew it wouldn't last, but for now, it was her only salvation.

LUKE HAD NEVER BEEN an emotional man, always fitting the mold of the dispassionate scientist. But as the woman left, and he looked at Mitch on the bed, he fought tears. *Keep busy,* he told himself, and he turned to the doctor. "If you could call and have arrangements made for the interment, I'll go through things in here."

Doc nodded, then turned to leave, the sadness of his task almost palpable.

Luke looked around the room. He couldn't believe Mitch was gone. He didn't know where the woman had come from, but he knew that she loved Mitch. And that shocked him. Mitch, the one who had women, but never stayed around for long. The one who never needed anyone. Luke wondered if Mitch had loved her and hoped he had. No one should have to suffer the grief she so obviously endured without being loved in return.

He reached for a dark comforter, tugged it up and over Mitch, then turned and went into the lab. He had to get all of the notes, all of the data, and he didn't have a lot of time to waste. He had to be back at the lab by this afternoon to do damage control. No one could know about this until he knew just what Mitch had found.

He took off his coat, went to the computer and booted it up. But when he tried to access the files, he was blocked by the flashing message: Enter Password. He'd never talked to Mitch about security and he was at a loss. He typed in word after word, but nothing worked.

When he sat back, frustrated, Doc came hurrying into the room. "Luke, you've got a call."

He turned to the older man. "Who is it?"

"Someone named Rupert. He says he's your lab assistant."

Luke stood. "What did he say?"

"He said he went in to prep the subjects for autopsies and—"

A crashing sound in Mitch's bedroom cut off his words. Luke turned. "What in the—" And as he looked at the bedroom door, he gasped, "My God."

HARLEY WENT TO HER ROOM, stood there for a moment, then knew where she had to go. She got her jacket on and went outside, into a day where dawn was just beginning to break. It was like the other dawn when she'd gone outside looking for Mitch. And that's what she was doing now.

He wasn't in the room by the lab. She knew that. As she trudged through the deep snow, she lifted her face to the sky streaked with pastel color. To a new day. A new world, actually—a world without Mitch in it. She made her way slowly into the woods and kept going until she broke out into the clearing with the rock where Mitch liked to sit.

The rock was bare now. Turned to the view, with its breathtaking vastness, she slowly sank down on the hard support of the giant piece of granite.

She sat there for a long time, waiting, hoping that being there would give her a sense of closeness to Mitch. That she'd sense him here, that his soul had lingered here in some way. But as she stared out at a world that showed no traces of life, she knew that it was empty. As empty as every other place would be for her now.

With that thought, she felt the numbness start to dissolve. She'd hoped and prayed that it would last, at least until she got back to L.A. and took care of things there. But her prayer wasn't answered. The numbness slipped slowly and insidiously from her, exposing the raw pain that she'd tried to hide from. And giving life to a burning, horrible rage that threatened to consume her from the inside out.

She hugged her arms around herself and rocked

slowly back and forth as rage and grief overtook her. Her crying wasn't quiet and deep, it was painful and came in great waves that shook her with the sobs. No pain had ever felt like this.

In a burst of agony, she stood and threw her arms out and screamed. The sound echoed back and forth in the open land, beating against her own ears and plunging into the agony inside her. She raged against life, against the fates that gave her Mitch then snatched him back from her. A horrible cosmic joke that had one shattering punchline: Mitch was gone. She'd lost him.

As the rage began to ease, dissolving into a place inside her where emptiness lived now, she sank back onto the rock and buried her face in her hands. She had the passing thought that she couldn't survive, but that gave way to reason. She'd survive. She might wish she wouldn't, but she would.

She'd survive to do what she'd promised Mitch she would do. She would love him for the rest of her life.

"Lady?"

The word came to Harley on the wind, the suggestion of a voice calling her name. She grew very still, her hands pressed to her face, and she listened.

Then it came again. "Lady?" Closer, clearer.

The numbness had gone, but evidently her mind was persisting on tormenting her. It was such a cruel trick, letting her imagine Mitch's voice. Hallucinations. Imaginings. Whatever she called it, it was madness.

A madness that persisted, until she tried to banish it as she pressed her hands hard against her eyes, then rubbed them roughly over her face. She sniffed back the tears, and opened her eyes to the whiteness of the world, where snow was beginning to fall softly from a darkening sky. A chilly wind was building, coming down the gorge from the east, and she knew it was time to go.

She'd come here to feel close, to have some connection with him, but she knew now that she was just tormenting herself. It only made the pain deeper and harder to endure. She had to leave, to get away from this place and try to learn to live with what had happened here.

But when she turned, the madness persisted, taking an even more painful turn. Through the softly falling snow, she saw a man in the clearing, a large man in a heavy jacket and a watch cap pulled low over gray-streaked hair.

He stood in the knee-deep snow, his hands in his pockets, his shoulders hunched into the wind. And his face was blurred by the falling snow and the failing light. Mitch. She swallowed hard and prayed the vision would go away, then prayed it never would.

She was imagining every detail of him, from the way he cocked his head to one side to the way he squinted as he studied her. His image was etched in her heart so deeply that it was there in front of her.

Then she saw the image move, slowly making its way toward her, and the closer it got, the more real it became. It had substance—the mist of his breath on the cold air, his hair ruffling in the breeze. The snow gathering on the shoulders of his jacket.

As the distance between them dissolved, Harley didn't move. She couldn't. She didn't know how far her imaginings could go, then she found out. He was five feet from her, near the edge of the ridge, and his voice drifted to her on the cold air. "Lady, I love you."

His last words. Words that sank into her soul. Tears were there again; madness, pure and simple, but she was beyond caring. Slowly, she went to him, closer and closer. Then he was filling her world, his ghost—his image, whatever it was— more real than life itself to her.

He cocked his head to one side, his hazel eyes narrowing, then said again, "Lady, I love you."

As the words echoed around and through Harley, she saw Mitch lift his hand, reaching out to her.

And he touched her.

Epilogue

Thirty-six hours later

"Lady, I am so tired," Mitch breathed as he saw Harley in the doorway of the room off the lab. "Doc just left to take Luke to the airport for a flight back to San Francisco, so he can clear out the lab and bring everything here."

Harley looked at Mitch, who was standing by the bed. It was the first time they'd been alone together since he'd found her in the clearing. Since that moment she'd found out he hadn't died, that they had another chance. Now that there was no one but the two of them, she felt oddly awkward.

She took in every detail in the low light. His hair was mussed, his jaw roughened by the shadow of a coming beard, and he was dressed only in his jeans. There was a Band-Aid on the inside of his left elbow, but other than that, he looked blessedly alive and healthy.

"The testing?" she asked without moving toward him.

"Done, as far as we can go with it right now."

"And?" She almost held her breath until he started to talk.

"I'm tired. I need sleep. I get out of breath." He smiled weakly. "Normal, disgustingly normal."

Wonderfully normal, she thought. "That's it? You don't know why that happened?"

"Just guesses. The serum caused the body to shut down, go into a sort of suspended animation, to facilitate healing. Trauma triggered it, we think." He ran both hands over his face, then raked his hair back, combing it with his fingers. "Dammit, I don't want to talk about this now. That's not why I told Doc to ask you to come down here." He came toward her. "That's not what I want now."

"What do you want?" she breathed.

"Oh, lady, if you have to ask me that, I'm very wrong about everything." He reached out and his hands cupped her face with aching gentleness. "I can touch you. I can hold you. I've got everything I ever wanted right here in my hands. I want you."

"I want you," she whispered, then walked into his arms. She knew she could stay here forever, lost in his embrace. She relished his hands moving on her back, the touch of his lips on the top of her head and the beat of his heart against her ear.

She realized that his heartbeat wasn't slow and

steady the way it had been, but racing, echoing her own. She slipped her arms around his neck and tipped her head back to look up at him. "I've missed you."

In the next instant he had her in his arms, and they were at the bed, falling onto the linens together, tangled in each other's embrace. Their clothes were gone and finally they were together, with no barriers. And Mitch touched her, his hands trailing over her, exploring her, the caress drawing responses from her that didn't come slowly. They exploded in her, mingling with a need for him that was overwhelming.

His kisses were deep and compelling, and his touch brought wave after wave of pleasure, until she was arching to him, begging for release. Suddenly he drew back and she opened her eyes, gasping, "No, Mitch, I..." But her protest died when she saw him over her.

His hazel eyes were glowing and his hair fell forward.

"Yes," she breathed, and lifted her hips to meet him. As he entered her, she arched higher. With each thrust she met, she felt her life falling into place with a perfection that defied description. Their bodies were in unison, rising and falling, joining together.

As the climax came, Harley wrapped her legs around his hips and held him in her until the feelings subsided. She drifted back slowly, the pleasure dispersing gradually. Then with a sigh, she felt Mitch leave her, and they rolled onto their sides, still facing each other.

He stroked her back and arm, then traced the line of her jaw with the tip of his finger. "I just want to look at you," he said in a low whisper.

"I thought I was crazy," she said, her voice preciously unsteady. "First Superman, then you in the snow, and I thought..." She took a shuddering breath. "I was sure I was insane."

He laughed, a rough sound that rumbled between them, and his hand gently cupped her breast. "Lady, the only way you're crazy is that you didn't run like hell when you first found out about all of this."

"I couldn't," she admitted. She tried to smile, but her expression faltered when he teased her nipple with the ball of his thumb. Sensations ran riot through her. "That's so wonderful...your touch."

"Oh, you have no idea how much I hated that part of all of this." His expression tightened for a fleeting moment as his hand on her stilled. "I don't know what's going to happen. If other side effects will show up, or if the serum is out of my system. I can't make any promises."

"Just promise to love me," she said. "That's all I need."

"That's far too easy. I'll love you forever, for

the rest of my life," he whispered. "And I could stay like this forever and be more than happy."

As he spoke, his words brought back reality. A reality she didn't want to face, but knew she had to. She covered his hand on her breast with her own. "Mitch, we can't...I mean, I can't. I have to go back to Los Angeles. I promised Ruth."

"With everything that's happened I forgot. You've decided what to do?"

"I'm doing what a wise man once recommended. I'm telling the truth and taking my chances."

"And if you lose everything?"

"Everything? It's a career, not my life," she said with stark truthfulness. This was her life—loving Mitch and being with him. "I'll survive."

"I know you will," he murmured as his hand moved from hers. He lifted himself on one elbow, his eyes narrowing slightly. "So you'll be leaving?"

"I have to."

"Of course you do," he said, but didn't touch her again. He studied her with that look, and she could almost feel distance growing between them. It grew wider when he said, "You have to do what you need to do. God knows, I've done what I had to."

She touched his arm, resisting the need to hold on to him with all her might. "I wish..." She lifted her hand to the roughness on his jaw. "I have to go. I can't just run away from it."

"Or course you can't." He studied her long and hard, then he shocked her by saying, "What if I go with you?"

Even as he said the words, Harley knew it was all wrong. "Thank you, but you can't come with me. I'm going to give interviews, and if anyone knew about you, they'd start digging. I can't ask you to do that."

"You didn't ask."

"I'm not asking," she said, and stroked his cheek, her hand barely steady. She felt desperate to break down the barriers he could start building with one look. "You can't be there, but I could come back here. If you want me to."

"I don't think you can do that," he said, and she felt a fear starting to replace all the heat and caring that she'd found with him.

"You don't want me to come back?"

"Oh, it's not me, it's Doc."

"What?"

"It's Doc. He's a good man, and I wouldn't do anything to compromise his standards."

She frowned at Mitch. "Or course not, but—"

He touched her lips with one finger. "The bottom line is Doc definitely won't put up with you coming back here, spending a few nights in this room with me, doing God knows what together, and us not being married."

She stared at him, then his words sank in. "Mitch, I thought you meant that..." She found a smile, and it felt so good. "Married? Us?"

"You and me, lady." His expression was slightly wary and she could feel him tensing. "Will you marry me?"

"Oh, yes," she whispered. "Yes."

He sobered, and when she would have kissed him, he gently held her back. "We have some problems. First of all, I don't know what's going to happen to me. I really don't."

"We'll face that together," she said, and meant it. No matter what, she'd be with him.

"Secondly, I'm staying here. I'm going to help Doc, then eventually take over his practice, and I'm going to keep working on the serum. This is where my roots are and where I want to settle down. It's home."

"Of course it is."

He looked confused. "You don't sound surprised."

"I figured it would come to that, sooner or later."

"Smart girl." He smiled, then said, "What about your career?"

"I might not even have a career after I go public,

and if I do, that's great. If I don't, I'll just keep going."

"Are you sure?"

"Yes, very sure."

He kissed her then, quickly and fiercely, then drew back. "Anything I missed?" he asked.

"Just this," she said, and she went to him, her legs tangling with his. "I know you're tired, but I'll be gone tomorrow, probably for a while. You can get plenty of rest while you plan the wedding." She kissed him and felt him responding. "And I'll be back as soon as I can get here."

"How soon?" he asked against her lips.

When his hand touched her, she sighed. "Very soon."

"Los Angeles is a long way from Crazy Junction."

She smiled up at him as he levered himself over her. "I'll fly."

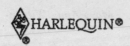

Not The Same Old Story!

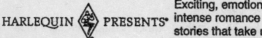 Exciting, emotionally
intense romance
stories that take readers
around the world.

Vibrant stories of
captivating women
and irresistible men
experiencing the magic
of falling in love!

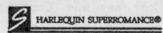 Bold and adventurous—
Temptation is strong women,
bad boys, great sex!

HARLEQUIN SUPERROMANCE® Provocative, passionate,
contemporary stories that
celebrate life and love.

 Romantic adventure
where anything is
possible and where
dreams come true.

Heart-stopping, suspenseful
adventures that combine the
best of romance and mystery.

 Entertaining and fun, humorous
and romantic—stories that
capture the lighter side of love.

Look us up on-line at: http://www.romance.net   HGENERIC

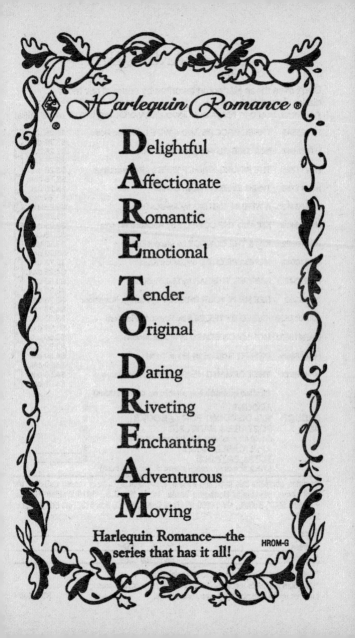

Harlequin Romance ®

Delightful

Affectionate

Romantic

Emotional

Tender

Original

Daring

Riveting

Enchanting

Adventurous

Moving

Harlequin Romance—the
series that has it all!

HROM-G

HARLEQUIN®

Don't miss these Harlequin favorites by some of our most
distinguished authors!
And now, you can receive a discount by ordering two or more titles!

HT#25645	THREE GROOMS AND A WIFE by JoAnn Ross	$3.25 U.S. ☐	
		$3.75 CAN.	
HT#25647	NOT THIS GUY by Glenda Sanders	$3.25 U.S. ☐	
		$3.75 CAN.	
HP#11725	THE WRONG KIND OF WIFE by Roberta Leigh	$3.25 U.S. ☐	
		$3.75 CAN.	
HP#11755	TIGER EYES by Robyn Donald	$3.25 U.S. ☐	
		$3.75 CAN.	
HR#03416	A WIFE IN WAITING by Jessica Steele	$3.25 U.S. ☐	
		$3.75 CAN.	
HR#03419	KIT AND THE COWBOY by Rebecca Winters	$3.25 U.S. ☐	
		$3.75 CAN.	
HS#70622	KIM & THE COWBOY by Margot Dalton	$3.50 U.S. ☐	
		$3.99 CAN.	
HS#70642	MONDAY'S CHILD by Janice Kaiser	$3.75 U.S. ☐	
		$4.25 CAN.	
HI#22342	BABY VS. THE BAR by M.J. Rodgers	$3.50 U.S. ☐	
		$3.99 CAN.	
HI#22382	SEE ME IN YOUR DREAMS by Patricia Rosemoor	$3.75 U.S. ☐	
		$4.25 CAN.	
HAR#16538	KISSED BY THE SEA by Rebecca Flanders	$3.50 U.S. ☐	
		$3.99 CAN.	
HAR#16603	MOMMY ON BOARD by Muriel Jensen	$3.50 U.S. ☐	
		$3.99 CAN.	
HH#28885	DESERT ROGUE by Erine Yorke	$4.50 U.S. ☐	
		$4.99 CAN.	
HH#28911	THE NORMAN'S HEART by Margaret Moore	$4.50 U.S. ☐	
		$4.99 CAN.	

(limited quantities available on certain titles)

	AMOUNT	$
DEDUCT:	**10% DISCOUNT FOR 2+ BOOKS**	$
ADD:	**POSTAGE & HANDLING**	$
	($1.00 for one book, 50¢ for each additional)	
	APPLICABLE TAXES*	$_____
	TOTAL PAYABLE	$_____
	(check or money order—please do not send cash)	

To order, complete this form and send it, along with a check or money order for the
total above, payable to Harlequin Books, to: **In the U.S.:** 3010 Walden Avenue,
P.O. Box 9047, Buffalo, NY 14269-9047; **in Canada:** P.O. Box 613, Fort Erie, Ontario,
L2A 5X3.

Name: _____

Address: _____ City: _____

State/Prov.: _____ Zip/Postal Code: _____

*New York residents remit applicable sales taxes.
Canadian residents remit applicable GST and provincial taxes.
Look us up on-line at: http://www.romance.net

HBACK-JM4

HARLEQUIN PRESENTS

HARLEQUIN PRESENTS
men you won't be able to resist falling in love with...

HARLEQUIN PRESENTS
women who have feelings just like your own...

HARLEQUIN PRESENTS
powerful passion in exotic international settings...

HARLEQUIN PRESENTS
intense, dramatic stories that will keep you turning
to the very last page...

HARLEQUIN PRESENTS
The world's bestselling romance series!

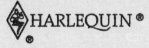

And the Winner Is...

You, when you pick up these great titles
from our new promotion at your
favorite retail outlet this February!

Diana Palmer
The Case of the Mesmerizing Boss

Betty Neels
The Convenient Wife

Annette Broadrick
Irresistible

Emma Darcy
A Wedding to Remember

Rachel Lee
Lost Warriors

Marie Ferrarella
Father Goose

Heartbreak RANCH

Four generations of independent women...
Four heartwarming, romantic stories of the West...
Four incredible authors...

Fern Michaels
Jill Marie Landis
Dorsey Kelley
Chelley Kitzmiller

Saddle up with Heartbreak Ranch, an outstanding
Western collection that will take you on a whirlwind
trip through four generations and the exciting,
romantic adventures of four strong women who
have inherited the ranch from Bella Duprey,
famed Barbary Coast madam.

Available in March,
wherever Harlequin books are sold.

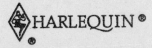

HARLEQUIN ®
®